Abby—Trouble in Tahiti

BOOK 7 IN ABBY'S SOUTH SEAS ADVENTURE SERIES

DON'T MISS THE OTHER EXCITING TITLES!

SOUTH SEAS ADVENTURES

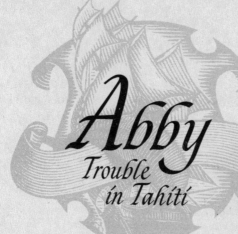

Abby
Trouble
in Tahiti

PAMELA WALLS

TYNDALE HOUSE PUBLISHERS, INC.
WHEATON, ILLINOIS

Visit the exciting Web site for kids at www.cool2read.com
and the Abby Web site at www.abbyadventures.com

ISBN 0-8423-3632-X, mass paper

Printed in the United States of America

11 10 09 08 07 06 05 04 03 02
10   9   8   7   6   5   4   3   2   1

WITH HEARTFELT THANKS TO SOME SPECIAL PEOPLE WHO BLESS MY LIFE: OSWALD CHAMBERS, WHOSE *MY UTMOST FOR HIS HIGHEST* KEEPS ME ON TRACK; JOSH MCDOWELL FOR *MORE THAN A CARPENTER*, WHICH HELPED CHANGE MY LIFE 18 YEARS AGO; JAMES DOBSON, WHO FAITHFULLY BROADCASTS WISDOM AND HOPE; KAY ARTHUR FOR *OUR COVENANT GOD*, WHICH TELLS OF GOD'S UNSHAKABLE COMMITMENT TO US; AND DR. KENNETH TAYLOR, WHO TRANSLATED THE BIBLE FOR YOUNG READERS, STARTED TYNDALE HOUSE, AND GRACIOUSLY ALLOWED ME TO PUBLISH THE ABBY SERIES.

THANKS ALSO GO TO MARK TAYLOR, RON BEERS, CARLA MAYER, KAREN WATSON, AND RAMONA CRAMER TUCKER FOR THEIR CONTINUING SUPPORT OF THE ABBY SERIES; PLUS THE MULTITALENTED TYNDALE KIDS FICTION TEAM, WHO FIND MY FLAWS AND FORCE ME TO IMPROVE!—ANDREA MARTIN, GINNY WILLIAMS, KAREN WATSON, LINDA WASHINGTON, AND RAMONA CRAMER TUCKER. BIG KUDOS ALSO TO TRAVIS THRASHER AND JULIE MIKOLAJCZYK, THE BEST CHEERLEADERS EVER! AND SPECIAL THANKS TO AMY AND AMANDA, MY A+ GIRLS, WHOSE ENCOURAGEMENT MEANS THE WORLD TO ME.

You will keep in perfect peace all who trust in You, whose thoughts are fixed on You!
Isaiah 26:3, NLT

Chapter One

OCTOBER 1848

Abby Kendall bent over, grabbed a handful of wet black sand, and rubbed it between her fingers. Raising her eyes in wonder at the sapphire lagoon, she inhaled the scents of this new tropical island. The salty sea wind carried the sweet fragrance of vanilla, which Uncle Samuel said grew wild. "We've arrived in paradise!" Abby gushed to Luke Quigley, her best friend. "Just look at that view of Tahiti." She turned and pointed inland, toward jagged mountain peaks, each one cloaked in rich green velvet and ribboned with silver waterfalls.

Luke chuckled as his dancing green eyes roved Matavai Bay's black-sand beach, where they'd landed a few minutes earlier. He nodded at Abby's nine-year-old sister. "Sarah loves this special sand for building castles."

"And Sandy loves it for digging," Abby added. Luke's eight-month-old, blonde-and-white pup was burrowing furiously into the dark sand, nosing for crabs alongside Sarah. *"Arrr!"* The pup's head came up suddenly, and Abby could see she'd found more than she'd bargained for. A two-inch crab had attached itself to her nose!

Sandy yipped and backed up, shaking her head to dislodge the crab, but it wouldn't budge. When the pup peered down her nose to get a good look at what pinched, her chocolate-brown eyes almost crossed with the effort.

Sarah and Luke doubled over in laughter, but Abby hurried to Sandy and batted the crab off her tender face. "Poor baby!" she crooned, kneeling next to the dog and giving her a squeeze. Sandy's plumed tail wagged in appreciation. "Shame on you, Luke Quiggley!" Abby chided. "I've a mind to stick a sand crab on *your* nose."

"Aw, come on, Abigail *Patience,*" Luke said with a chuckle. "It's been a long sail from Indonesia and we were cooped up for weeks. Have some fun!" He scooped up a small piece of driftwood and threw it for the pup. "Let's take Sandy on a walk so she'll forget her troubles."

Sarah, her white-blonde hair bright in the sunlight, glanced up from her work of digging a castle moat. "I'm too busy to go."

Abby fell into step next to Luke, her cinnamon curls dancing down her back. She glanced back at her mother, Charlotte Kendall, and Lani, the lovely Hawaiian woman who now traveled with them. Together they sat on a beach blanket.

"Speaking of busy," Abby said, her eyes on the

two women, "Lani's chattering like a magpie about this being the perfect place for her upcoming wedding. I'm glad she and Ma are busy planning. We'll have time to explore Tahiti."

Luke shook his head in amusement. "I've never seen Lani acting so girly before—she's tied up in knots over all those details. I plan on staying out of her way until it's over."

Abby grinned. It was clear the romance of Lani's big day was lost on Luke.

The soft *swish* of waves spilling onto the beach, then receding, blocked out Lani's animated voice as Abby and Luke walked down the curved shore toward a distant point. Coconut palms swayed in the breeze up the dunes. Colors seemed bolder here, the air more perfumed. Abby could see tall Mount Orohena rising in a dramatic peak, wearing a garland of swirling mist. A faint rainbow arched above a rain-spent cloud.

Luke slowed his longer strides to match her shorter ones. Abby was glad he understood the leg weakness she'd inherited from her ma and let her rest when she needed it. Now Luke followed her gaze. "I wonder if there's a pot of gold at the end of that rainbow," he teased.

With each step, Abby's feet squished in the warm dark sand. "Gold or not, it's heavenly here," she said in wonder. "It's even more beautiful than Hawaii, and you know how I feel about home." Indeed, she and Luke had fallen in love with the

Hawaiian islands they'd already seen: Oahu, Maui, Lanai, and Kauai. And even though Abby's family now lived aboard their trading ship, the *Kamana*, they all thought of Hawaii as home base.

But as she stood on Tahiti's beach, Abby knew she could fall in love with this island, too. She already enjoyed the cool feeling of the lacy surf that rushed up to kiss her bare toes. And she couldn't wait to draw the view of sharp mountain peaks she could see from the beach.

Luke tossed a piece of driftwood into the waves. Water splashed onto his blond sun-streaked hair and freckled nose. He wiped it with the back of his hand. "Uncle Samuel said the marine life is richer in Tahiti than in Hawaii. It has something to do with cold water welling up from the bottom of the lagoons."

"There are more fish—and they're more color-ful," she said, remembering the short rowboat trip from the *Kamana* to shore in the glasslike water. She glanced at their schooner now as it bobbed on the bay. Duncan MacIndou, their Scottish captain, was belowdecks with Thomas Kendall, Abby's pa, and Uncle Samuel. They were still taking inventory of the silk, rice, and spices the *Kamana* carried for the upcoming trade they hoped to make in Tahiti's Papeete Harbor. They'd traveled thousands of miles since Duncan had purchased the abandoned ship in San Francisco and formed a trading company with the Kendalls.

Luke began to walk again and Abby fell into step next to him, shaking sand from her lavender dress skirt with one hand. Cinnamon curls danced down her back as she glanced back at her mother, Charlotte Kendall. Ma and Lani, the lovely Hawaiian woman who now traveled with them, sat talking together on a beach blanket.

It was during a trip to Kauai that they had discovered Lani, Duncan's half sister. And now she was engaged to marry Abby's biologist uncle, Samuel Kendall. One of the main reasons they had come to Tahiti was to give Lani the wedding of her dreams.

"I think Lani wants the wedding to take place soon," Abby said with a sigh.

"There can't be much to do, since there's no one to invite but us," Luke said in his practical way. "But I'm beginning to think Lani would like to invite everyone who lives here."

Abby laughed and squinted up at him. "But Luke, you're missing the point. Weddings are celebrations . . . and so romantic."

Luke only rolled his eyes.

"Who could have guessed," Abby said, ignoring him, "a year ago, when your Aunt Dagmar wouldn't let you leave California with us, that we'd be sailing the South Seas? Remember how we always wanted to go traveling together?"

Abby thought back to the day she'd met Luke, four years ago, when he'd come to California as an orphan to stay with his aunt. Abby's family had offered the lonely boy love—something Aunt Dagmar seemed unable to give—and Abby had been rewarded with a best friend.

"Are you still drawing everything in your journal?" Luke asked.

"Yep." Abby looked inland again at the soaring peaks. "In fact, there's a quality of light here that makes colors more vibrant. I wish I could paint what I'm seeing. Chalk and pencils can't capture those shimmering blues and greens."

"Maybe we could buy you some paints," Luke said.

"Even if we could find some," she said, "I've never learned. Painting takes a special skill. I'm not sure I have it."

They walked on in silence for another minute before Abby suggested they head to the distant point.

"Okay, as long as we get back in time for lunch," Luke said with a wink. "A 15-year-old boy needs lots of food to grow."

"You're not 15 *yet*," Abby challenged, her sapphire eyes snapping. "Right now, we're *both* 14." She cast him a smug glance, but the truth was, she only had 10 more days to enjoy "catching up" with him in age.

"Ha!" Luke countered. "Just 10 more days, Abigail *Patience* Kendall, and I'll be a year ahead of you again." He sighed with satisfaction and then sniffed the breeze. "I smell something cooking!" Hurrying ahead of her, he pointed. "Look, a woman up ahead is tending a fire. She's cooking . . . bacon! Do you think she'd share it with us?" Abby saw the dark-haired woman bent over a cook fire. Smoke rose lazily from it, and blankets were spread out nearby. Like the Kendalls, someone else had come to enjoy this tranquil bay.

Below the busy woman a burly Tahitian man walked in the surf. Every now and then he would gaze seaward, as if looking for something.

Abby shook her head. "If you're that hungry, let's head back to our picnic. No doubt the Tahitians are as generous as the Hawaiians, but I hate to see a grown boy beg."

They turned around and retraced their steps, soon rejoining Sarah. Sandy began digging again, but she backed up and growled this time when she encountered a crab.

Smiling at the puppy's antics, Abby glanced up and noticed the Tahitian man had drawn much closer. Now he was only 10 yards off, still gazing out to sea as he hiked through the foam.

Sarah stopped molding wet sand into a castle turret. "I wonder what that man's looking at," she murmured.

Abby shaded her eyes from the bright sun. The man had a tall, powerful build and a handsome face. He wore a green wrap of *tapa* cloth, secured around his waist.

Abby looked beyond the Tahitian to the darker blue water. "I think someone's swimming out there." She could just make out an arm splashing. Whoever it was, they were in deep water.

Sarah stood up and walked toward the surf. The Tahitian man was just a few feet away now. Abby joined Sarah. Through the foaming water Abby noticed a knife sheath strapped to the man's calf. For a brief moment she wondered if he could be dangerous, and she put a cautious hand on Sarah's shoulder. But he glanced at them and smiled, showing white teeth.

Abby grinned back as he nodded to her, but Sarah kept moving forward into the surf, almost barring his path. "Look," she said to both Abby and the stranger. "There's more than just a swimmer out there . . ." Sarah swallowed and pointed. "I see a shark!"

Abby's eyes frantically sought out the swimmer. *There!* A large triangular fin kept pace about 30 feet behind the swimmer. The instant Abby saw the size of the fin, she knew the shark must be huge.

"Luke!" Abby shouted. "The rowboat—"

Sandy started barking as Luke leapt to his feet, racing toward the small craft drawn up on the sand. But the Tahitian man didn't hesitate. He ran into the oncoming wave and dived under the glassy curl, then pitched into the deeper water with the strong, sure strokes of an athlete.

8

Abby couldn't believe her eyes. *He's swimming toward the shark!*

She raced after Luke, who was dragging their ship's rowboat into the foaming waves. Soon they had it bobbing on the water, and he held it steady while she gathered her long lavender skirt and climbed in. Luke pushed it farther out, the water sloshing over his waist, then threw himself over the gunwale. Settling onto the wooden bench, he gripped both oars and began heaving with all his might. The little skiff leapt forward and plowed through the next wave. Abby's eyes widened as she turned to peer ahead.

Don't let us be too late, God! Abby prayed.

As the boat drew near the Tahitian man, Abby could see he was almost to the swimmer—a woman. She was treading water, her lovely copper face almost ashen with fear.

"Where's the shark?" Luke asked.

"There!" Abby shrieked. Its huge fin closed in on the woman, who turned to face it as it circled her in a deadly game.

Just then the man dived beneath the surface. Abby's heart raced. No doubt the cold-blooded fish was readying for the kill. Could that stranger save the woman?

When the man resurfaced, his right hand came up first. Sunlight glinted off the silver knife blade as he positioned himself directly in front of the woman.

The shark fin plowed straight through the water toward him, then disappeared beneath the sea. In the next second the man disappeared, too!

Abby let out a bloodcurdling scream.

Chapter Two

Luke rowed with all his might. Thirty seconds later they drew up next to the woman, who was still bravely treading water. The swells sloshed against the boat as she reached for its side. Abby looked down at her and shouted, "There's blood in the water!"Abby grabbed the Tahitian woman's arm as she clung to the side of the skiff. Luke dropped the oars and helped Abby lift the woman aboard.

As soon as the swimmer was in the boat, she peered over the side, searching the depths. "Tunui!" she screamed, her voice laced with desperation.

Abby saw bubbles rising from the darkness below. The water churned and suddenly Tunui, the Tahitian man, shot up from the depths, gasping for breath. He grabbed the side of their little craft, tossed the knife onto the floorboards with a clatter, and swung one leg over the side. The boat tipped crazily with his weight. As he pulled himself up, a gash on his upper arm bled freely. Moaning in pain, he let go and slipped under the sea's surface again.

"No!" The woman rose frantically, tossing the

boat into spasms of rocking. Luke reached her and pulled her back down onto the narrow bench.

"I'll get him," he promised.

"Don't go in, Luke!" Fear pulsed through Abby. She didn't want her best friend swimming with that monster below.

But Luke didn't pause. He dived overboard and swam down toward Tunui. Through the clear water, Abby could see him reach the injured man. She held her breath as she watched the unfolding scene.

Blood in the water is bound to draw more sharks!

But the next instant Luke broke the surface with Tunui in tow. He pulled him toward the skiff while Abby and the swimmer reached out to help the injured man aboard.

As Luke grasped the gunwale to pull himself in, Abby saw the man-eater again—this time just below Luke's legs! In another second he could be shark bait! She panicked and lunged for Luke, dragging him into the rowboat.

"It's okay, Abby. The monster's dead from his knife," Luke said, dripping and breathing heavily. He nodded toward Tunui.

Adrenaline pumping, Abby stared over the side and saw the huge fish was indeed floating belly-up. The ocean's surge had moved it to a few feet below the surface.

"A hammerhead!" Abby said with a shudder.

The shark was 12 feet long and its wide, hammer-shaped head was clearly visible. Blood trickled from a cut in its white chest as it floated upside down.

Abby couldn't help but stare at the deadly beast.

"Tunui, you're hurt."

Abby turned to see the Tahitian woman reach out a hand toward Tunui's wounded arm.

"It is but a small price to pay," he said quietly.

The swimmer's dark eyes sought his. "I thank you for your courage."

Tunui gazed back at her. "It is a privilege, my—"

But she hushed him with a finger to her lips and spoke in her lilting Tahitian language for a minute. When she was done, she switched back to English. "Now we must get to shore and take care of that cut."

"First we'll catch a shark," Tunui said as he unwound the rope at the back of the rowboat with his good hand. The giant fish was now drifting belly-up near the stern.

Luke whistled. "Those hammerheads are sure ugly," he said, pointing to the grotesque head with the underslung jaw and wide-open eyes jutting from the sides.

Abby watched Tunui reach into the water and loop the boat's mooring line around the shark's tail. "Let's get to shore before more sharks arrive," she said as Luke took up the oars again. "My mother can bandage that cut," she offered Tunui.

At those words the black-eyed Tahitian woman smiled for the first time. Her lovely eyes lit up, but it was more than her outward beauty that struck Abby. In spite of her bedraggled appearance—the wet wraparound clothing and dripping black hair tied back—and the fact that she had almost been killed by a shark, joy radiated from her. An inner beauty seemed to shine through.

"The Lord was good to send you in our moment of need," the stranger said serenely. "I'm Aimata, and this is my good friend, Tunui."

"You're a Christian!" Abby said excitedly. "Luke and I are Christians, too!"

The woman inclined her head toward Tunui. "Most of our people have walked with God for many years now—since the missionaries came from England decades ago."

"I'm so glad," Abby said. "Is that how you learned English, too?"

"Yes," Aimata replied quietly.

"By the way," Abby said, "it was my sister, Sarah, on shore there, who saw the shark, not me." Abby pointed. "She's got the 'eagle eyes' in our family."

"Ah, I must thank her right away." The woman toyed with her necklace, a gray silk cord from which a pendant hung. The lustrous orb shimmered in the sun like quicksilver.

"What is that on your necklace?" Abby couldn't help but ask.

"Ah, it's a Tahitian black pearl. Lovely, yes?" Aimata asked.

"Yes," Abby answered, thinking how it seemed to reflect an inner light—just like its wearer.

Luke continued to pull on the oars until they were close to shore. Abby saw that Ma, Lani, and Sarah had spotted them. Soon all three were hurrying toward them to help beach the rowboat.

Luke and Abby jumped out and pushed the boat ashore. As Aimata and Tunui got out, they were greeted warmly until the 12-foot hammerhead at the back of the boat floated up onto the sand. Sarah screamed and jumped back, while Sandy the pup growled and barked furiously at the threatening fish that moved slightly in the water that rushed up the beach.

After the excitement had calmed down, Lani ushered their guests to the blanket on which to sit. Ma clucked with concern when she saw Tunui's wound. Digging through the lunch basket, she took out a cloth and ripped it into strips. Then, getting a bowl and water, she carefully began to wash his arm.

Meanwhile, Aimata beckoned to Sarah to come sit beside her. Sarah's silky, white-blonde hair blew in the soft trade winds as she cocked her head in curiosity.

Aimata, who looked about Ma's age, smiled at Sarah. "I want to thank you, little one. Your good eyes saved me."

Sarah beamed at the compliment.

"I'm grateful you were here to help," Aimata went on. She raised her hands to the back of her neck, untied the silken gray cord, and then retied it behind Sarah's neck.

The opalescent jewel was magnificent against Sarah's pale skin.

Ma glanced up at Sarah and stopped her work of binding Tunui's cut. "Oh, Aimata, we're honored, but we can't accept that—it, it's too lovely. Sarah doesn't need to be rewarded."

"Ma," Sarah said sweetly, "if this will make Aimata happy, you don't want to cheat her of joy."

Aimata laughed. "No, you should not go against my wishes. And yes, this will make me very *oa oa*— very happy," she agreed. The giant black pearl caught the sunlight, shimmering green and blue like the aquamarine sea. "I insist that she take it and remember me by it. And be glad the Lord gave you 'eagle eyes,' Sarah, so you can do good works."

Sarah threw her arms around Aimata's neck. "Thank you!"

Seconds later Abby was surprised to hear the quiet Tunui speak. "You've done much more than you know, Sarah."

Before further words were spoken, Sarah pointed up the beach, where an outrigger canoe was landing. "Look, a canoe just beached." Two men pushed it up the sand and headed toward them. As they came near, Abby could see that one was older, the other a teen.

Both were dark-skinned, lithe, and approached with ready smiles. The older of the two had bushy eyebrows and busily took in each person as he came near. Recognition flashed in his brown eyes. *"Ia orana!"*

"That is one of our Tahitian greetings," Aimata explained. "Mahoi, *aita,*" she said, directing her words to the new arrivals. For a brief minute Tahitian words flew from her mouth. Then her speech slowed as she switched to English and introduced each one in Abby's party. "This is Mahoi," she told them, "a dear and trusted friend—and his son, Rahiti. They are the best pearl divers on the island."

Mahoi, whose bright personality was evident in his merry face, laughed. "I am glad to make your acquaintance," he said. "Are you staying long?"

"Just 'til we can have Lani's wedding to Uncle Samuel," Sarah blurted out before Ma could shush her.

"Oh?" Aimata said, interest showing on her face.

Lani blushed and glanced out toward their ship, the *Kamana.* "It's been a dream of mine to come here," she explained. "Since I am half-Hawaiian, I've always wanted to visit the birthplace of my ancestors. And," she finished in a rush, "have my wedding in the most beautiful place on earth."

Aimata smiled in pleasure. "And so you shall," she said with an assurance that promised help. "Mahoi's family and I will do all we can to assist you. Tomorrow Rahiti can take you to Papeete Market, where you can pick out what you require for that most special day."

Mahoi bowed. "My wife, Ruth, and I will also be pleased to help. You must come and meet her at once. She is full of ideas," he said, eyes twinkling, "and loves to share them."

Aimata smiled. "They can meet her tonight, Mahoi, for they are coming to your home for a shark feast." She turned to Abby's ma, Charlotte, and Lani. "You see, I often spend time at the home of Mahoi and Ruth. It is large, and we are close."

"Please, Ma?" Sarah asked anxiously.

"We'd be grateful, Aimata," Ma said. She gently finished tying the strip of cloth on Tunui's arm and then warned him, "You must rest your arm to let the wound heal."

Tunui stood and bowed his head gratefully. "Thank you, Mrs. Kendall."

"We are staying down the beach, beyond the dune," said Aimata. "Come just before nightfall, all right? You will hear the gourd drums and see the fire pit from the beach here."

"Did you say dinner tonight?" the ever-hungry Luke questioned.

"Yes," Rahiti said with a laugh, "and very good *ma'a*—food!"

Abby thought Luke's eyes almost glazed over with contentment as Mahoi and Rahiti spoke to Aimata, offering to take care of the shark meat since Tunui was injured.

Then Tunui and Aimata walked away, down the beach.

Mahoi pointed at the shark, still washing in waves. "We will have a fine dinner tonight. Who caught the great shark?" But before Abby could explain, Mahoi's eyes fastened on the pearl at Sarah's throat. "Where did you get this, little one?" He reached out to touch it.

"Aimata gave it to me," Sarah said with a contented sigh. "It looks awfully expensive."

Abby blanched at her comment, but Mahoi only nodded solemnly and murmured, "You are right. It is an especially rare and perfect pearl. But how did she come to give it away?"

Sarah launched into the story of how she had spied the giant shark, and Mahoi's face darkened with concern. "How blessed we are that you arrived in time." He and Rahiti went to inspect the shark and untie it. Returning to their canoe, they gathered items and then began the work of preparing the giant fish. Soon huge gray slabs of shark steaks were piled into net bags, which the two Tahitians hoisted onto their shoulders. "Come to my home tonight among the coconut palms so we may honor your family," Mahoi said.

Waving good-bye, Rahiti shouted, "Come hungry!"

Luke leaned into Abby. "I wonder what hammer-head shark tastes like?"

She grinned. "It's got to be better than bird's nest soup. Remember eating that in Indonesia?" She shuddered, remembering the salty, unusual-tasting broth.

"Aw, it wasn't so bad," Sarah said in her little-sister, know-it-all tone. "Especially when you picked out the feathers."

Chapter Three

At twilight the entire crew—Ma, Pa, Abby, Sarah, Uncle Samuel, Lani, Duncan, Luke, and Sandy—began their hike up the beach toward the fire they could see in the far distance. Pa rubbed his hands together in eager anticipation. "I'm ready for a barbeque, Charlotte, and all kinds of Tahitian dishes."

Duncan adjusted his black eye patch and winked at Abby with his good eye. "And with any luck, the Tahitians will serve *poi*, Luke's favorite dish." Laughter rang out. Everyone knew Luke hated the Hawaiian dish that looked like purple paste.

A few minutes later, as they began climbing a dune that led to a forest of rustling coconut palms, Abby slowed. With her inherited leg weakness, climbing was hard. She could see her ma's steps slowing down, too. Up ahead they could see the fire blazing brightly near the dune cliff.

To their left the sun was sinking rapidly into a calm sea. Clouds on the horizon gathered the last rays of light into an apricot glow. "Look," Abby said. They turned to view streaks of scarlet and copper splashed across the sky. Murmurs of approval broke out.

But the sound of drumbeats beckoned, and they pressed on. Making their way toward the fire beacon, they saw woven *tapa* mats spread out. The tantalizing aroma of shark steaks sizzling over the blaze drew them close.

Mahoi tended the meat while Rahiti, who played the gourd drum, raised a hand in greeting. "Welcome!" Both Mahoi and Rahiti wore head garlands of shiny green leaves. "Sit! Sit!" Rahiti urged as a woman and a girl came forward. Both smiled and wore plumeria- and hibiscus-flowered wreaths around their heads. Yellow, peach, and white, they were fragrant crowns. "This is my mother, Ruth," he explained, "and my sister, Orama, which means 'flame' in Tahitian. Orama is well named—she is a firecracker!"

Abby instantly sympathized with Rahiti. Obviously he had a sister just like her own!

"We are so happy to have you," Ruth said, greeting Ma and Lani with warm hugs.

Ruth and Orama wore mission-style cotton dresses that were called muumuus in Hawaii. Orama, who looked about Sarah's age, carried fragrant leis over her left arm. But these leis, Abby noticed, were much shorter than the typical Hawaiian lei.

"Mother and I made these for each of you," Orama said as Ruth set one on Abby's head. Then

Orama draped a green-and-white, sweet-smelling strand of flowers on Lani's head. The garland fit perfectly, like a crown. "I used our favorite flower, the *tiaré* blossom."

"Mmm," Lani said as she breathed in the pungent scent, "it reminds me of gardenia."

"And it makes you look like a princess," Uncle Samuel said. For a moment the two stared affectionately into each other's eyes. But the spell was broken as Sandy bounded over Samuel's knees to chase Sarah and Orama as they ran off.

Rahiti beckoned Abby and Luke away from the fire, where the grown-ups chatted. "Come, I'll show you our home." The two set off eagerly behind the friendly youth as he led them from hut to hut. These rooms had no walls—only mat flooring, coconut-trunk support beams, and *pandanus*-leaf roofs.

"Why aren't there any walls?" Abby asked.

"Under this forest of palms," Rahiti explained, "we are protected from everything but the largest storms. We love to feel the cool breezes—this is the traditional home of our people. Separate buildings for separate functions. Here is the *fare tutu*, the kitchen." There two women, busily preparing food, looked up and smiled.

Rahiti led them to the next building. "This is the *fare tamaa*, our eating area. But tonight we will be out under the stars. Our sleeping quarters, the *fare taoto*, is over there. Of course, the other building is for bathing. When a bad storm comes, we move our sleeping mats to that house," he said, pointing, "because it has walls for protection."

Luke whistled. "Your house goes on for quite a distance."

Rahiti smiled. "The land and buildings have been in my family for generations. They were given to us by King Pomare I. Here we live and eat and come home from our sea hunts."

"You mean when you go fishing in your canoe?" Luke said.

"Yes, and when we go diving in the secret places for black pearls."

Luke looked wistful. "I would love to see what you see under the water. . . ."

"Do you want to go with us sometime?" Rahiti asked.

"Really?" Luke turned to Abby. "Doesn't that sound great?"

Abby's mind took flight. "Imagine finding a pearl as lovely as the one Sarah's been given! How I would love that."

Rahiti sobered. "That is one of the finest in all the world," he said. "Such a gift from Aimata should be treasured above all others."

For a moment they were silent, and something unspoken hung in the air. Abby wondered if Rahiti knew a secret he couldn't—or didn't want to—reveal.

Then Rahiti continued, "If you do want to go pearl diving, I can arrange it. Perhaps tomorrow?"

Abby glanced at Luke. "We would love to!"

"Then you should spend the night here in our home. At first light you and Luke can join my father and me."

Luke grinned. "What a treat."

"The real treat is just about ready," Rahiti teased. "Let's go eat."

Soon the families were gathered near the fire pit on the *tapa* mats. They were joined by Aimata, who also wore a floor-length, floral-print mission dress. "Where is Tunui?" Abby asked Rahiti before she sat between Aimata and Lani.

Rahiti shrugged. "He often leaves at odd hours, running errands and picking up items from the palace."

After Mahoi prayed over the meal, the women brought trays of coconut-steamed rice; platters of oranges, mangoes, guava, and papayas; steamed sweet potatoes; fresh-baked breadfruit, as well as French bread and butter; grilled shark steaks; bowls of lilac-colored *poi;* and for dessert, vanilla custard.

"Luke," Abby teased, "there's plenty of poi for a second helping. . . ."

His lips twitched as he tried not to smile. "Abby, you're so thoughtful, but I've got to save room for dessert."

Conversations and laughter rang out. The night had darkened, but the stars and moon that rose over the bay brought enough light to see by. A gentle trade wind drifted in from the sea.

Once Aimata had finished asking Lani and Uncle Samuel about their wedding, Abby leaned toward her. "Why do you have French bread here on Tahiti?" Abby asked. "I didn't see it on any of the Hawaiian islands we visited."

A rueful smile flickered across Aimata's face. "It is delicious, is it not? But how it came to be here is a sad story.

"Our people have a proud heritage—one of kindness toward each other," she said as the conversations around the fire quieted. "Here in Tahiti there has always been enough food for all. No one worked hard to live. All we needed grew in abundance. The papaya, the mango, breadfruit, and *taro*. Mulberry and *pandanus* from which we made our clothes, the *pareus,* and these mats," she said patting the one on which she sat.

By now everyone stared at Aimata, listening to her story. "Of course, there were *tabus,* rules to follow that sometimes limited our freedoms. And, I am sorry to say, there were times when people were sacrificed to island gods. For a long time we did not know how wrong that was . . ." Aimata's words trailed off, and Abby saw her sadness.

"But God in His kindness," she said more energetically, "sent us missionaries from England who taught us that He did not require human sacrifice. In 1812, King Pomare II was on the throne. He was the first of our people to believe in the Christian God of love and justice. And as soon as he did, the entire nation turned from the old ways and embraced new faith in Christ."

Abby sat enthralled. Her mother had given them a lesson about Tahiti as they traveled on the *Kamana,* but hearing it from a real islander was much more interesting.

"Alas," Aimata continued, "ever since the days of Captain Wallis, the first sailor to come to our shores in the 1700s, disease has been taking our people. You see, we knew almost no disease—as hard as that might be to believe. And we had no natural defenses against the diseases the sailors brought."

"So what happened?" Luke asked.

Aimata's smile disappeared. "Now there are not many Tahitians left. Eighty years ago there were 150,000 of us. Today there are only 7,000." She shook her head and tossed a small piece of wood onto the fire.

Mahoi now spoke, his face clouded with emotion. "We have lost many loved ones."

Aimata nodded. "My baby brother was one. . . . And then six years ago the French arrived. They wanted to own our island, and we have struggled against them ever since. For two years we fought them like rebels—hiding, attacking, winning some battles, losing others. . . ." Aimata gazed into the fire for a minute. "But they won about a year ago. Now the French tricolor flag flies over Tahiti's palace. Their priests have come, their bakers, their chefs, and others. And that is how we have come to have French bread in the marketplace in Papeete."

Mahoi frowned.

Rahiti glanced at him and said proudly, "My father fought bravely. And Tunui also led raids against the French."

"Yes," Aimata said, smiling, "they are both Tahiti's heroes."

Mahoi sighed. "Those days are gone. But today let us lift our hearts and not be sad. We are grateful, are we not? For this day was a good day."

Aimata nodded graciously. "That is the only way to overcome our disappointments. When difficult things happen, we must look for things to be grateful for."

Rahiti stepped away to gather the large gourd drum from its spot nearby and then returned to the circle. He began a beat that was soothing, and Mahoi led the other Tahitians in a song about their land. Abby closed her eyes and was swept into the timeless music, which spoke of love for their island.

When the song finished, she opened her eyes.

Aimata said softly, "You see, Abby, even in the toughest of times, there's always something to be thankful for."

"But are you angry at the French for taking over your island?" Abby asked.

"Some people *are* angry," Aimata answered with a sigh. "But living in anger will only bring bitterness. So I look for the good God gives. And today

Sarah saw the shark, and you, Tunui, and Luke came to my rescue."

"But sometimes being thankful is not easy," Mahoi put in.

"Yes," Aimata agreed. "Sometimes when I see the French flag snapping in the breeze where our Tahitian flag should be, I still struggle, Abby."

The Tahitians had gone through so much, Abby thought, and still they looked for the good things God was giving them. Tears pooled in Abby's eyes. She wished she was as brave as Aimata.

When a tear spilled down her cheek, Abby quickly wiped it away.

But Aimata reached out and touched Abby's face. Aimata's dark eyes shone with friendship. "Your tears show how much you care, Abby. *Mauruuru,*" she said with tenderness. "I thank you."

Chapter Four

Dawn had barely broken when Abby stretched, yawned, and sat up on the *tapa* mat on which she'd slept. At first she couldn't understand why the ship wasn't moving in the eternal ocean swells. Then it came flooding back—they'd accepted Mahoi's invitation to sleep in his expansive home. Now she saw the ocean from the open-sided hut. Sarah and Ma were still sleeping beside her.

She rose and wandered toward the cliff face, near the fire pit. Rahiti was up, sipping something. "Coffee, Abby?" he asked.

"Yes, please." On board ship, when it was her turn at watch, she had learned to drink it with a little sugar. He quickly returned with a mug.

"We must leave now. Father is already down at the canoe waiting for us, and I have orange muffins packed for breakfast." Rahiti held up a leaf-wrapped package.

"Then let's go wake Luke," Abby said, excited.

Abby held on to the sides of the wood outrigger canoe as Rahiti and Mahoi paddled through the swells toward Venus Point, north of Matavai Bay. They had left Mahoi's home at dawn, with Abby dressed in one of Aimata's *pareus* so she could go pearl diving. Luke wore his old cutoff pants and a shirt.

As much as Abby loved being on the sea, she couldn't help thinking of the large hammerhead that had almost killed Aimata and Tunui yesterday.

Still, she reminded herself, running into a hammerhead wasn't likely to happen again. And, after all, being on the water offered a splendid view of Tahiti, with her soaring mountain peaks and aquamarine seas. Then Abby's gaze fell to the bottom of the canoe and the rocks tied to long ropes. At the other end of the ropes were green glass balls, which Rahiti said floated on the surface. Luke had said he couldn't wait to grab a stone and jump overboard, plummeting to the seabed in his search for the elusive black oysters. She, too, was eager to find a gorgeous, glistening black pearl. But the thought of giant sharks still made her nervous.

An hour of paddling brought them to a tiny lagoon fringed with a coral reef. The canoe easily slid over the top of it. "Do you think a big shark can get through that reef as easily as we did?" she asked Mahoi.

He grinned at her. "Yes, they are smart. But don't worry. I carry a knife, and I will be close by."

Mahoi steered them to the north side, where they soon anchored the canoe and tied net bags around their waists to hold the oysters they collected. "Here," Mahoi said to Abby, "you will need this knife to loosen the oyster from its bed. They stick on hard. Pry it up like this, okay?"

Abby took the pocketknife and tucked it into the bag.

Rahiti scanned the depths. His short black hair shone with coconut oil in the early morning sun. "It's only about 20 feet deep here. The rock will take you straight down. As soon as you get to the bottom, slowly let the air out of your lungs so you don't float to the surface, okay? When you have to come up for air, you can get back down again by pulling yourself along the rope attached to your stone. You will save energy that way."

With those words Rahiti stood up with a large stone in his arms, then jumped into the water. Luke *yahooed* like a kid just out of school, and Abby grimaced. "Don't wake up the sharks," she scolded. But Luke just grinned and leapt in after Rahiti. Abby watched him sink through clear waters until he was almost to the bottom.

"Your turn," Mahoi said encouragingly to Abby.

Abby's stomach was tied up in knots. "I'm . . .

I'm going to wait awhile," she told Mahoi. "You go ahead without me."

He smiled sympathetically and then dived overboard without a stone. Abby could see him pulling his way down on the line Rahiti had dropped. Small and large fish cleared out of his path as he descended, and then Abby was alone. She cast a look about the lagoon. On the surface all looked serene. Maybe hammerheads didn't frequent this bay.

Screwing up her courage, Abby stood up carefully and picked up the last stone. She closed her eyes, said a prayer for safety, then jumped.

Swoosh! Bubbles surrounded her as she fell slowly through the lagoon's cool water. The heavy stone tipped her so that her head and arms plunged first, her legs and feet now trailing. Abby opened her eyes just before she reached the sandy bottom. She dropped the stone and immediately floated upward in the surging water.

Grabbing the line, she hung on. Suddenly Luke was there, smiling at her. When he let out a tiny stream of bubbles, Abby remembered to do the same.

He motioned for her to follow, and Abby swam behind him. Although the salt water stung her eyes a little, it was worth it to discover a whole new world. Abby was shocked to learn there were sounds beneath the sea—soft clicking noises. And the colors! Pink and yellow corals were everywhere. And orange-and-black fish darted around her as if they were curious. A big blue fish, at least three feet long, swam just yards away. They floated back and forth with the ocean's surge, as if they'd abandoned themselves to the sea's rhythm.

How wonderful it would be to paint this scene, Abby thought.

Luke didn't seem as interested in the view as in his goal. He'd gone right to work on a rock formation, searching for oysters.

Abby followed behind him for a few more seconds, then followed as he shot upward for a breath of air. With all the air gone from her lungs, she didn't float as well, and she had to swim hard to reach the top. By then her lungs were burning for oxygen. She burst above the sea and gasped. Luke grinned at her until a swell sloshed him in the face. But that didn't dampen his spirits. "It's great, isn't it?" he said. Then he took a deep breath and dived back down. Abby followed.

They found the line floating between the glass ball and its anchor, then pulled themselves downward, heading straight to the rock. Abby saw black oysters cemented to their stony perches. Luke quickly began dislodging one. When he pried it loose, it flipped up, then began sinking. Abby caught it and stashed it in her bag. Luke smiled without opening his mouth, then kept at it. Another one came loose, then another. Abby pocketed them in Luke's bag. It was time, then, for a breath of air.

This time Abby beat Luke to the surface and headed back down first. She began prying an oyster but found it to be harder than it looked. Finally it came loose, just as Luke opened his bag and dropped two in. He moved over for Abby, drawing close to the entrance of a small round cave. When Abby was ready to return to the surface, she pulled on Luke's shirt. He glanced her way, gripping the edge of the cave opening to keep from floating up. Suddenly, out of the cave shot a giant moray eel, mouth open and lunging toward Luke's fingers!

Though she couldn't move as fast as the eel, Abby yanked hard on Luke's shirt. His fingers slipped off the ledge and the eel twisted out. As Luke caught sight of it, he kicked backward. It flowed out of the cave like a sea snake. Instantly Luke pushed off the bottom and headed toward the surface. Abby, stunned by it all, watched the moray eel pour out of its den in a long fluid movement. Its evil-looking mouth still gaping, it kept coming out until Abby thought it must be six or eight feet long.

And it headed right after Luke!

Its mouth was wide open and its thick knifelike tail lashed through the water behind Luke's bare foot. Abby wanted to scream, but instead she pushed upward in an attempt to help. She kicked hard while trying to get the pocketknife out of the net bag around her waist. Up toward the surface she flew, but it seemed the closer to the surface Luke got, the less eager the moray eel was to give chase.

Suddenly it turned and headed back down—

almost colliding face-to-face with Abby. She jerked the knife upward, but the blade wasn't open! Yet the eel spun away from the movement and kept going. Abby burst through the surface, gasping for breath.

Luke quickly swam over. "You okay?"

But she couldn't speak. Her heart hammered in her rib cage. She knew from Uncle Samuel that moray eels had a nasty bite. They'd even been known to hold swimmers underwater.

Luke led her to the canoe and then helped her get in over the side. Once there, she insisted he join her.

"Nah," he said. "This is great! Have you ever seen such beauty? Don't worry—the eel's more scared of me than I am of it. . . ."

Abby couldn't believe her ears. That horrible eel hadn't even dampened his enthusiasm.

"You rest," Luke said, "and I'll be back in a little while."

"Luke, wait!" she cried out in warning.

But he was gone.

Abby hoped it wasn't for good. But as the seconds turned to minutes, she worried. Then she got angry. How *dare* he leave her all alone, to worry that he might be facing new dangers. After all, he'd almost been attacked by a shark . . . and now by a moray eel. It was too much, all within two days!

When Abby caught sight of him surfacing a dozen yards away, he grinned crazily at her and waved his bag of oysters.

But by then she was really angry. *Let the eel have him!* she thought as he dived beneath the swells again.

Twenty minutes later Luke's teeth were chattering with cold and his eyes red from the salt water as he pulled himself into the canoe. "It's a lot of work," he gasped out, "but I got 12 oysters."

"You risked your life for 12 oysters?" she snapped, her voice brimming with impatience.

He just looked at her with raised eyebrows and grew quiet.

A few minutes later, Mahoi and Rahiti finished their work. After tossing their heavy bags over the side, the two pearl divers climbed skillfully into the outrigger canoe.

The return trip flew by with a steady wind filling their sail. Soon they were dragging the canoe up onto the familiar black sand of Matavai Bay. "Let's open the oysters now," Luke urged.

Mahoi and Rahiti had captured 42 black oysters.

"If there are no pearls among them," Mahoi said, "at least we will have oyster stew for dinner!"

"Mmm," Rahiti murmured. "A good morning dive, and an even better evening to look forward to."

"Why won't there be pearls in every oyster?" Luke asked, as he followed their lead and inserted his knife between the two shells to pry the oyster open. Abby did the same with the few that she had found.

"Because," Mahoi answered, "few oysters produce our famous black pearls. Pearls are only created when a little grain of sand gets in between the flesh of the oyster and its shell. That grain irritates the oyster so it coats the sand with its mother-of-pearl. Over time the sand is coated again and again with that beautiful shell. Finally, after several years, that irritant is turned into a precious pearl."

"So the oyster takes something bad and ends up turning it into something good," Luke said thoughtfully. "That's amazing." He bent back to his work on one large oyster and gasped as he lifted up the meat. "Abby, look!"

She leaned over and gazed at a magnificent pearl—large and perfectly round. The shiny silver orb was tinged with an aquamarine sheen. Forgetting her irritation with him, she cried, "Oh, Luke, you've done it!"

Mahoi nodded. "That one is of great value," he said soberly.

Rahiti came over and patted Luke on the back. "Beginner's luck, my friend!"

Luke's eyes gleamed with his find. He stuffed it in his pants' pocket and went back to work on the other oysters.

"What are you going to do with it?" Abby asked him.

"Save it for now, and maybe sell it later," Luke answered.

"Maybe when we pry these other oysters open," Rahiti added, "we'll find more pearls and we can sell them in Papeete this afternoon. Then we can buy your friend Lani a very nice wedding gift."

Chapter Five

Two hours later they were winding down the dirt road toward Papeete City in Mahoi and Ruth's buckboard wagon. Ma and Ruth were on the seat with Rahiti, who was driving the roan horse, and Lani was in the back with Abby and Luke, talking about all the types of food, clothing, and flowers she couldn't wait to see.

The sun was warm but the air still relatively cool for the tropics since it was October. The hot humid season hit in November. Before them lay Papeete Harbor, with perhaps 40 ships at anchor in the wide protected bay. Abby quickly noted the French man-of-war also at rest in the harbor. The main thoroughfare of the city, fragrant with pink and yellow plumeria, was close to the water. Blossoms colored every home and business with the orange, red, and white blossoms of hibiscus, bird-of-paradise, and *tiaré*.

As Rahiti directed the horse with gentle urgings, Abby realized the youth had a special way with horses. He had to, since the horse stayed calm despite the bustle on Boulevard Pomare—people walking in the street, children running, shopkeepers sweeping doorsteps. But there were also groups of French soldiers milling about on street corners. With their crisp dark blue uniforms and sheathed sabers, one could hardly ignore their military presence.

At the entrance to the marketplace, Rahiti tied the horse to a tree. "This is Papeete Market," he told them as he leapt out and helped Ruth and Charlotte down. "This is where ships unload and merchants sell their wares. Father sells our black pearls here, but today I will do it for him." He was referring to the two pearls out of the 42 oysters that they'd harvested.

Abby was amazed that the harvest was so small, but when Rahiti held out his calloused palm with the silvery black pearls captured there, she drew in a quick breath. "They are beautiful," she said, picking up the shiniest one. "Look how it glows in the sunlight."

Rahiti smiled. "That's called *luster*. The more luster a pearl has, the more valuable it is." Abby could see that each pearl had a particular sheen to it. This one had a green cast, the other a blue, but neither of them was as lovely as Sarah's or Luke's. Rahiti picked up the lopsided bluish pearl. "This pearl is imperfect and not as valuable as the other, but I will still be able to sell it today at the marketplace."

"I hope you do," Abby said, her blue eyes almost as bright as the pearls she prized.

Ruth already had a basket on one arm, with pencils and paper in it. "We're going to search for everything Lani needs. This will give her an idea of what she wants. Rahiti, be back here at the wagon by the middle of the afternoon."

Rahiti turned to Abby and Luke, looking pleased with the arrangement. "I must buy items for my family. But we will have time for other things, too." As he led them into the marketplace, Abby stared at the brightly colored scarves and long *pareus,* the long cloths used to make wraparound Tahitian clothing; tables laden high with limes, grapefruit, oranges, sweet-smelling vanilla beans, and dark yams; baskets of freshly baked bread; hand-carved wooden dishes, gourd pots, and drums; a man holding the leashes of five fat pigs for sale; women hawking baskets of eggs and crates of chickens; a table of crudely made toys, among them *roarers.*

Rahiti explained how a roarer worked. "When you swing it around quickly," he said, showing them, "it makes a whistling noise." As it spun overhead, the small hollowed-out gourd sounded similar to the noise Luke made when he blew in the top of a narrow bottle.

The street seemed to go on for a mile. It was flooded with people carrying baskets as they shopped. Sailors dressed in white duckcloth pants and blue shirts milled about on shore leave from whalers and trading ships. There was even a trader from South America selling green parrots in cages. "We need to sell our cargo here," Abby told Luke.

Luke nodded. "Your pa is planning to sail into Papeete Harbor to unload soon."

Rahiti quickly purchased the items needed and dropped them off at the wagon, under burlap sacks. "Now what do you want to see?"

"The place where you sell the pearls!" Abby crowed. Luke grimaced and Rahiti laughed at him.

"I need to go there anyway to sell our 'big catch.' Why don't we go past the fish market on the way there? You can see the catches of the morning, Luke. By this time much has been bought already, but it's still pretty interesting."

Luke brightened. "Sure."

Rahiti led them down toward the harbor where fishermen had sold their catch to the market men. Laid out on wooden planking were all types of fish Abby had never seen before and others she recognized from their own fishing lines off the *Kamana*: bluefin tuna, mahimahi, ono. There were squid and octopus for sale, and even freshwater eels from local rivers.

Abby urged them to move quickly through the fishy-smelling area. Then they headed toward the jewelry merchant.

As they walked, Rahiti shared a little about his job. "Two or three days a week I work in the queen's palace. I help with the gardens, fix things, and sometimes do special shopping for our monarch."

"The queen's palace?" Abby asked. "Don't you have a king, too?"

"No, Queen Pomare IV is our monarch. She's been on the throne 21 years now."

"Sounds interesting," Luke said. "Can we see the palace?"

"You want to meet the queen?" Abby teased.

"He can't," Rahiti said. "The queen is not here but is visiting friends. Some think she's on Mooréa." He pointed out toward Papeete Harbor. "See the island in the distance? It's Mooréa—a place even more beautiful, some say, than Tahiti."

Abby's mouth dropped open. "That's hard to imagine. I'd love to see it. . . ."

"I can't take you there," Rahiti said, "but I can get you into the palace. It's not far from here, and the Pomare treasures are on display. Besides, I'd like to show you where I work."

Luke rubbed his hands together. "Let's go!"

Rahiti looked at Abby for confirmation. She nodded. "That sounds fun."

"First, give me a minute with the jewelry merchant over there," Rahiti said, pointing to a small wooden storefront. "I'll be back soon."

As they waited under the shade of a plumeria tree, Abby nudged Luke. "Can I see your pearl?" She wanted to hold the glistening gem in her hand again. It was so shiny, almost as perfect as Sarah's. How she wished she'd been the one to find it!

Luke heaved a sigh as he dug into his pants' pocket. "Girls and their pearls," he said. "Where's that pearl ring you got from Violet's dad when we were in China?"

"I put it away for special occasions. It's too valuable to wear every day." She watched Luke dig into the other pocket, then turn to her with a blank expression.

"It's not here."

"What? You managed to lose it already? How could you be so . . . careless?" Abby felt her face flush. All the frustration she'd felt with him over the diving incident earlier in the day came back with a vengeance. How could he lose such a valuable treasure? It was worth a lot. "How could you be so . . . so *stupid?*"

The expression on his face made her instantly regret her words. But at that moment Rahiti returned, and Luke looked away from them both. "Ready to go?" Rahiti asked.

Abby bit her lip, sorry she'd used that terrible word. But it was too late to apologize now. Not with Rahiti looking on. "Yes, let's go," she said quietly.

Rahiti shot off through the crowd, leading them away from the harbor and through the rustic town of Papeete. They hiked south for 15 minutes, and Abby was glad when they slowed.

A huge grass and plumeria tree park surrounded

the palace, a large wooden structure ornately deco-
rated. Springs of water welled up in two places on
the palace grounds, where Abby saw people busily
drawing water with wooden buckets. In the distance
Abby made out another home. Rahiti followed her
gaze. "That's the French Commissioner's resi-
dence," he said grumpily. Above both residences
the French blue-white-and-red flag flew.

Leading them to the palace front steps, Rahiti
greeted two large Tahitian guards. *"Ia orana,"* he
said with a smile. The guards greeted him back in
Tahitian, and Rahiti led Abby and Luke inside.
"Sign the guest book," he told them, indicating an
open book and quill pen on a marble table in the
foyer. Then, leaning close to Abby, he added, "We
must be careful not to run into Chief Ono. He's the
queen's cousin and often acts as regent when the
queen is away. But he is nothing like her. He gets
angry very easily."

Abby smiled and whispered, "I understand. We'll
walk softly and try to be invisible."

Soon they were whispering their *oohs* and *ahhs*
as Rahiti led them through palace rooms. Royal
feather robes, along with ancient weapons and
helmets, many adorned with long red tail feathers
from tropic birds, were on display. "Those feathers
are considered royal emblems," Rahiti explained.

Visitors from around the world had given gifts to
the royal Pomare family, and many of these items
were also displayed: Chinese vases and urns; Louis

XIV French furniture; intricately carved paddles and *tiki* statues from neighboring islands in the South Pacific; and paintings from foreign dignitaries. Most interesting to Abby, though, was a large red-and-white flag mounted on one wall.

"Our Tahitian flag," Rahiti said quietly. "This is the last one that flew above the palace." He gazed at it for a moment, then said softly, "Come on, I want to show you something. As long as we don't run into Chief Ono, it should be okay." He led them to the east wing of the palace and down a short corridor that opened onto a well-lit sitting area. Windows overlooked a lovely flower garden. Several chairs, a credenza filled with books, and several potted plants were arranged so people could enjoy the view. Two hallways joined this area, both ending before an ornately carved door.

Suddenly they heard footsteps approaching from the adjoining hallway. Rahiti's brown eyes widened. "The chief! This way!"

Following his lead, they kneeled behind the large urn, chair, and ferns. The footsteps rang out purposefully in the hallway, then slowed. Abby peeked out a fraction of an inch and almost gasped. It was Tunui! He was looking over his shoulder, one hand on the doorknob of the ornate door. When he saw no one else around, he opened the door and entered.

Abby frowned. Why was he sneaking around the palace? she wondered. Rahiti looked over her shoulder and sighed softly. Turning to him, she whispered, "Why is Tunui here?"

"He works here, too," Rahiti replied.

"What's in there?" she asked.

"Those are the queen's quarters," he said nervously.

"Why would he be going in there?" Luke whispered.

"I don't know the answer to that—"

Just then voices came from the queen's room. "What are you doing here?" they heard Tunui say.

"Cleaning. Do you see this dust?" a woman answered harshly.

From the exchange Abby sensed that both Tunui and the parlor maid were surprised to encounter the other. Indeed, it did seem odd that a maid would clean with the door closed.

But before Abby could ponder further, Tunui ushered the young maid from the room and left also. Abby, Luke, and Rahiti waited several minutes more before getting up.

"We must get going," Rahiti finally said anxiously. "But you can take a quick peek. We will leave out the back way, through the kitchen. There is less chance that way of running into anyone but the cooks."

Abby and Luke gazed silently into the queen's quarters. A huge canopy bed dominated the room. Double-glass-paneled French doors occupied one wall that overlooked the garden. "It's lovely," Abby gushed, admiring the rich dark woods of three dressers, an armoire, and gilt-edged mirrors. One drawer on the smallest dresser was open just an inch, but Abby didn't mention it because Rahiti already seemed disturbed. Quietly she shut the carved door and turned to him. "What is it?" she asked. "Is something wrong?"

He glanced at her with mild surprise, then shook his head, as if to drive a thought from it. "Oh, it's just that there's a rumor that has been bothering me. . . ." He paused.

"You can tell us," she urged.

"You won't discuss it?" When they both said no, Rahiti sighed. "I've heard there's a spy in the palace—someone collecting information."

"A French spy?" Luke asked, his dark eyebrows creasing.

"Or a Tahitian who's turned traitor for money," Rahiti admitted.

"But why?" Abby asked.

"I guess the French would like to know what's really going on since the war," Rahiti concluded.

"Do you have any hard facts?" Abby asked.

"No. Maybe it is only a rumor," Rahiti said. But his face showed he felt otherwise. "Let's go." He led them toward the back of the palace, then stopped short in the hallway outside the kitchen. Abby heard someone shouting. A pot clattered.

Turning toward Abby and Luke, Rahiti looked desperate. "It's Chief Ono!" he whispered, sounding panicked. "I don't want to run into him—not when he's angry!"

Abby found herself sprinting behind Rahiti to the left, down a long narrow hallway. Rahiti tried several doors, all of them locked. The shouting from the kitchen grew louder. A dish crashed to the floor. Footsteps sounded. Rahiti's eyes raked up and down the narrow passageway for a place to hide. Abby's scalp prickled with fear as she, too, searched for a way out.

"Look!" She pointed toward a nearby door. Hanging on a nail next to the door was a black iron key. She grabbed it and inserted it in the lock. It turned—just as the kitchen doors burst open.

They rushed into the room and silently shut the door.

Chapter Six

"Bonjour."

The French word hung in the air as Abby, Luke, and Rahiti stared openmouthed at a dark-haired man in a painter's smock. When he stood up and made a gallant bow to Abby, she saw that he was medium height with a pleasant face. His blue eyes seemed to sparkle with interest at their arrival.

"Hi," Luke ventured. "Who are you?"

The man put down a brush and smoothed his moustache. "I am Jean-Paul Gabois, cartographer or mapmaker and, as you can see, artist." He gestured with a shrug toward the canvas that sat on the easel before him. "And who are you?" he asked curiously.

As they introduced themselves, Abby noticed that to his right, a wooden table was littered with at least 20 glass canning jars—a rainbow of liquid colors in the bottom inch of them. The room smelled strongly of oil paints and other chemicals Abby couldn't name. She glanced to the window. It was open, and leaning back in a chair next to it was a

Tahitian youth about Rahiti's age. He appeared to be sleeping.

"Vatu!" Rahiti said loudly. "What are you doing here?"

Startled, Vatu sat up and the chair crashed down onto all four legs. "Guarding the prisoner," he said with a nod toward Jean-Paul.

"But he's locked in!" Rahiti said.

"Windows be having no bars, and I be hating this job," he muttered.

Abby was already wishing for a breath of fresh sea air. "Can you breathe all right in here?" she asked the artist.

Jean-Paul smiled at her, his bright blue eyes crinkling a bit in the corners. "There ez no cross breeze. But do not worry for me, *mon amie*. When I am *fini* with these paintings, the horrible little man will let me go, *oui?*"

Rahiti's black eyebrows pulled down into a line. "Who locked you up here?"

"A nasty bully named . . . Chief Ono. I get the feeling he does not like the French, *oui?* And he ez taking his frustration out on me. . . . But I am almost done with the first of the two portraits he demanded of me—King Pomare II and his wife."

Abby couldn't resist the urge to peek at the canvas. As she came around behind him, she gasped at its impact. A handsome man stared at her, as if he were standing there in person. The quality of light and color the French artist had captured was so real, it was breathtaking. When Abby looked down at the bottom of the easel shelf she was amazed to see a lovely black-and-white pencil sketch from which he'd done the portrait. "Oh, my," she said, "you have brought him to life!"

He cocked his head at Abby with a slow grin. "You think so?" he said, pleased with her compliment. *"Oui*, it will do. But it ez not what I'm here for. Soon, when I am *fini*, I will fly the coop." He laughed from his belly, and Abby and Luke couldn't help but join in.

"How have you come to be locked up here? What crime did you commit?" Abby asked.

"Ah, *mon amie,* if only I were a writer I could pen a book!" He swished his brush in some liquid and dried it with one of the many dirty rags off the floor.

"I sailed to the South Pacific to meet my destiny," Jean-Paul answered, winking playfully at Abby and Luke. "But I had the misfortune of meeting Chief Ono at the home of my ship captain when I first arrived. When he discovered I could paint, he invited me here for a royal dinner. I came as a free man but I have yet to leave. No, I did not commit any crime, except that I am French and my countrymen have plucked Tahiti like a ripe peach." He shook his head in exasperation.

Luke, who had joined Abby in gazing at the painting, looked shocked. "They can't just lock you up for no reason!"

At that moment Vatu stood up and crossed his skinny arms over his chest. "Rahiti, you're not supposed to be here. This be a secret. Chief Ono wants these paintings finished for the queen's return. And no one's supposed to be knowing about Jean-Paul here. So you go—take your friends and leave."

Abby was about to turn and go when she saw the sadness in Jean-Paul's blue eyes. She just couldn't leave him here, locked up like a criminal! He'd done nothing wrong. "I . . . I'm an artist, too," she began, hoping to cheer him. "I mean, not like you! I just do pencil sketches now, but someday I want to learn to paint."

"Then come back and visit me, *mon amie,*" Jean-Paul said kindly. "And I will teach you while I do the next painting, *oui?*"

"Really?" Abby asked excitedly.

"I am most serious. I would enjoy your company."

Abby turned to Rahiti, but he shook his head. "Let's go," he said.

She glanced back at Jean-Paul with a hopeful smile. "I'll be seeing you . . ."

He bowed his head graciously, but just before Rahiti closed the door, Abby ventured one last look. Jean-Paul was staring down at his hands, his face no longer that of a playful gentleman. The mask had fallen, and Abby could see the lonely man in its place.

"It's totally unfair," Abby said as they headed across the palace grounds together.

"I don't understand it," Rahiti admitted. "The queen would never condone this, but then she's not here. . . . However, I can see Chief Ono doing this to get her favor when he presents the portraits to her."

"Boy, I thought the French were bad," Luke said. "But this proves you sure can't lump people together. It's what's in each person's heart that motivates him."

"And look at Jean-Paul," Abby said. "He's a wonderful Frenchman." She turned to Rahiti. "Is there anything you can do for him?" she asked as they headed up the street toward their waiting wagon.

"I can't stand against Chief Ono on my own," Rahiti said sadly. "He has too much power in the queen's absence. And at this time I don't even dare tell anyone. Please keep quiet about this, especially if we're to have any hope of helping him."

"What about going to the French authorities? They won't be happy about a French citizen being unfairly imprisoned," Luke said.

"True," Rahiti admitted, "but I cannot go to the French. I would be considered a traitor by my people."

By now they were nearing the area where they'd left the horse and wagon.

"I understand," Abby empathized. "You just fought a war with them and lost. But maybe you can take me back to the palace. I'd like to cheer up Jean-Paul."

"Vatu—his guard—is nice enough, but he's also Chief Ono's nephew. So I don't know if I'll be able to get you in to visit," Rahiti replied. "Vatu might not let us—"

"But we can try," Abby pleaded. "Can't we?"

Chapter Seven

"Whoa, boy," Rahiti called out to the horse the next morning.

Abby was excited. If Jean-Paul had really meant what he said, this would be the day of her first painting lesson. Ma had smiled when Abby had told her about getting a lesson from a master painter and had waved her off with a basket of freshly made banana muffins.

Today Luke had offered to help the men—Pa, Uncle Samuel, and Duncan—sail the *Kamana* into Papeete Harbor. Abby knew that, starting tonight, the whole family would be back on board ship for their sleeping arrangements. Not only would they be closer to shopping for Lani's sake, but also closer to the palace and her painting lessons.

Rahiti leapt down from the wagon, helped Abby down too, then tied the reins to a tree behind the palace. "Let's head in through the kitchen. I know I tried to go through them last time," he said with a chuckle, "but Chief Ono almost never bothers with the cooks." Abby grabbed the basket of muffins and followed Rahiti up the back porch steps, where there was no guard.

It was the perfect moment to arrive, she realized. Just after lunch with a few hours before dinner preparation, the kitchen was not only quiet but empty of cooks. Vegetables and fruit lay out on wide wooden tables, perhaps for the evening meal. The ticking of a regulator clock seemed loud as they tiptoed through the large room.

Midway down the hall they found the black key in its place. Rahiti grabbed it and unlocked the door. They walked in on a surprised Jean-Paul.

"Mon amie!" He seemed genuinely happy to see their smiling faces.

"I brought you some muffins," Abby said.

Jean-Paul came toward her and bowed. Vatu sat up at attention, looking hungry.

"Here," she said, hurrying to Jean-Paul, "I hope you like them. Ma added coconut for a bit of Tahitian flavoring."

Jean-Paul lifted the yellow dish towel covering them and inhaled. A rapturous smile spread across his handsome face. *"Oui,* still warm. They shall be perfect." Then he turned and spoke to Vatu. "A chair, if you please, for the young lady . . ."

Vatu jumped up and hurried over with his own chair for Abby. She sat down and looked intently at the painting Jean-Paul was just finishing.

"Come on," Rahiti urged Vatu, "let's find something to eat in the kitchen. You deserve a breath of fresh air."

"All right," Vatu said, lifting an iron handcuff off its hook on a wall. He clamped one end around Jean-Paul's ankle, the other around the table leg above the crossbeam.

Jean-Paul's eyes narrowed. Abby and Rahiti exchanged concerned looks before Rahiti turned to leave.

"I be tired of being in this room . . ." Abby heard Vatu say as the boys shuffled out of the room.

Jean-Paul raised an eyebrow and smoothed his dark moustache with one hand. "You are ready for your first painting lesson, *oui?*"

Abby's eyes glowed. "I am! I'm hoping I can use what you teach me to make a special present for Luke's birthday."

Jean-Paul picked up his brush again and began to speak as he worked on the background of the king's portrait. "I will teach as I work," he said. "And when we finish this one, I will show you how I mix the paints with oil. Tomorrow I will begin the portrait of the king's wife and you shall learn as I go. You can come back each day, *oui?*"

Abby swallowed. "I'll try," she promised.

"Good," he said with a nod. "To make something look realistic, we must have the shadows and high-lights we see in real life, *oui?*"

Abby nodded, thinking it was amazing that the

artist had made the painting come alive through shadows and highlights.

Jean-Paul continued. "In this picture, the light comes from the side of the king. So we make shadows here and here, where the light does not directly hit," he said, pointing with the brush. "I add black to the color I'm using to darken it and make a shadow under the arm. This ez called the *cast shadow,* because no light hits this part of the king."

Jean-Paul held a palette in his left hand and dabbed the brush in the different colors. "On the other side of the king, there ez more light," he said, pointing to the pencil sketch. "This ez called *reflective light,* and I add white to the color to lighten it." Then he launched into a discussion about the width of brushes and the purpose of each type. "Often, I make my own brushes," he explained, "from a bit of horse hair. My papa taught me how to do this."

"He is an artist, too?" Abby said.

"*Oui,* but he has never painted portraits professionally. He ez a cartographer, a mapmaker. One of the best in all of France. One of the most precise because he verified all his measurements on the ground and checked them in the air."

"What?" Abby asked, confused.

He smiled. "It was the French who invented the first lighter-than-air machine. My grandpapa flew one back in 1802. Ah, he was a true adventurer, one of the first men to soar above the clouds. How I loved him, Abby!"

"And he taught your father to fly one?"

"*Oui!* And my papa taught me. So I, too, want to be a cartographer. That ez how I learned English—I studied in Great Britain for two years." Jean-Paul leaned toward Abby and whispered a secret, "That ez why I packed up my papa's flying machine and brought it with me to Tahiti."

"One of those flying balloons is here?"

"At the captain's house. Captain Chevalier brought me here in his ship and unloaded all my supplies at his home above Papeete before he sailed away. It runs on hydrogen gas now, but later I plan to convert it to a hot-air balloon that burns coconut fibers—they're plentiful in the South Pacific. It was when I came to the palace for dinner that Chief Ono imprisoned me for his own selfish purposes—to find favor with the queen through my portraits. Unfortunately, Captain Chevalier had already sailed on by that time, and I had no one to help me." Jean-Paul sighed heavily. "I thought once I got here I would be free as a bird to soar above the seas and travel throughout the South Pacific, mapping and drawing for a book."

Abby's heart went out to him. "It must be hard to be caged like a bird instead."

Jean-Paul gazed down at his palms. "Sometimes I am close to despair. Once I tried to leave through the window at night, but there ez a guard posted there in the evenings."

"Your whole family is adventurous," Abby said,

hoping the change of subject might do him good. "Tell me about your grandpapa."

Jean-Paul smiled. "He was kind. White hair all over his head. Very smart. A fine Christian man. He liked to say, 'The Lord has a reason for everything.'" Jean-Paul shook his head. "I don't know if that's true or not. My papa did not believe in God at all, much to my grandfather's disappointment."

"Do you?" Abby asked.

"Perhaps. There may be a God who created the world. I don't know. But if He did, then why don't we see any evidence of Him? Perhaps He wound the world up like a watch and then left it to tick on its own. That's not what Grandpapa believed. As a young lad I remember hearing him say, 'The eyes of the Lord roam throughout the earth seeking to strengthen those whose hearts are fully committed to Him.' . . . It's funny I should remember that now. I suppose it ez because my heart needs strengthening. *Oui,* that is it. Right now it feels like a deflated balloon."

"Jean-Paul," Abby said, "I will pray for you. Your grandfather was right. God is watching and I know He cares."

The artist smiled softly and playfully brushed the tip of her nose with his paintbrush. "You are also kind, like my grandpapa. But his nose was never blue, like yours."

Abby grinned.

"Now, back to our lessons." Then she listened

intently as he described everything he was doing while he painted. The lesson went on for at least an hour, until the boys returned. Then Jean-Paul declared he was done for the day. "But you will return on the morrow, *oui?*" he asked Abby.

"Yes, and thank you." As much as she'd enjoyed her lesson, she was suddenly eager to look for the *Kamana* in the harbor. She missed Luke. When Jean-Paul had called her kind, it had wrung her heart. She hadn't been kind to Luke about losing the pearl yesterday.

Abby left Jean-Paul's room with Rahiti and hurried through the kitchen. Several cooks, wearing white starched aprons, were chopping vegetables when the two hurried through. "*Ia orana,*" Rahiti called out to them as he hurried Abby toward the back door. They stopped their chopping and looked curiously after them, then shrugged and returned to their work. Abby and Rahiti chuckled as they made their escape and headed around the side of the palace.

Abby realized that they were now on the side of the building where Jean-Paul's room was located. It was the same view she'd seen from his window. "Let's peek in and surprise Vatu," she said. Rahiti grinned with anticipation as they hurried soundlessly toward the only open window on that wall.

But no sooner had they arrived than they heard loud voices. An angry voice carried over the distant sound of horse traffic on the road near the harbor. And the voice sounded familiar.

Rahiti motioned for her to duck down under the window and stay still.

"You are not working fast enough! She will be back before the week is out," the enraged voice shouted. "Do what I command or I will make your life hard, painter!"

Abby's mouth tightened with frustration. *Chief Ono—the scoundrel! Wasn't it enough that he'd already imprisoned Jean-Paul? Did he have to yell at him, too?*

But Abby's thoughts were interrupted by Jean-Paul's response. He was furious, and Abby caught part of what he was shouting. ". . . no right to keep me locked up! I'll tell the French counsel, and you will pay for this kidnapping!"

"Oh no," Rahiti whispered, "that will only make Chief Ono decide to hold him long—"

There was a crashing of glass. Abby's head shot up to peek inside. Chief Ono had apparently smashed the butt of a whip down on the glass-covered table, knocking some of Jean-Paul's paint jars from their perch. Now the chief stood close to Jean-Paul, his face reddening with anger. He was a large muscular man—though not as tall as Jean-Paul.

When Chief Ono raised the whip as if to strike Jean-Paul, Abby gasped. Tahitian words spilled from the outraged chief until he must have realized

Jean-Paul did not understand. Then the chief switched to English, shouting at the top of his lungs, "You swine! *Fiu!* I'm fed up with you French! You will stay here until I allow you to go free. No one knows about you and no one will. You will see where the real power lies in Tahiti. Not with the stupid French. Not with the queen either. The power lies with me!"

Abby ducked as Chief Ono stormed out of the room, slamming the door so hard a plaster cross fell from the wall and shattered.

Poor Jean-Paul! Now there was no guarantee that he would be freed when the second portrait was done. What torture for an adventurous man. Abby's heart went out to the artist.

God, she prayed, *I know You can work all things together for good—even when things look bleak. So please show Jean-Paul that You are here. Give him hope!*

Chapter Eight

"Oh, Lani," Abby exclaimed the next day, "it's beautiful!" She ran her fingers over the shiny white silk. "And it will look gorgeous against your skin."

Abby and Lani were in the galley of the *Kamana*, a bolt of expensive silk laid out on the table. The family had spent the night with the ship moored in sheltered Papeete Harbor. Abby had wanted to talk with Luke the previous night since she knew she owed him an apology. But he'd gone to bed early. Abby got the distinct feeling that he hadn't gone with her to see Jean-Paul yesterday because he was trying to avoid her. So she had decided to wait to talk to him until he seemed in a better mood.

"Your ma and I picked it out from the silk in the hold this morning," Lani explained. "And I just got a note from Aimata. She says that she's asked two seamstresses she knows to come tomorrow to sew it according to any design I want. Can you imagine? It makes me feel like a princess."

"You'll look like one, too," Abby said, staring at

her aquamarine eyes and the long mahogany hair that fell to her waist. Uncle Samuel had found a wife who was beautiful inside and out.

Lani shook her head in wonder. "Aimata is so helpful and generous. She says she's paying for my dress to be sewn as a wedding gift."

Abby held up a box of dress patterns. "Have you picked a pattern yet?"

"No. Let's go through them and decide right now!" Lani said.

"I don't have to meet Rahiti until later this afternoon," Abby said, "so we have time." Ma and Sarah were off shopping for supplies. Luke had gone fishing with Mahoi, but Rahiti had stayed home because he had to work at the palace later today, while the men were in town trying to sell some cargo.

For an hour Abby and Lani sat side by side in the slightly swaying galley and pored over designs and ideas. By the time the men, Ma, and Sarah came back, Lani had decided on the style of her wedding dress. Abby shooed everyone out of the galley and showed Ma the style. "This close-fitting waisted gown with the full skirt and short train," Abby said, handing Ma the drawing. There was a slight scoop neck and three-quarter sleeves, which would be perfect, Ma said, in the warm tropics.

"What about a veil?" Ma asked Lani, her eyes shining almost as much as the bride's.

"I'm going to wear a garland of blossoms," Lani said. "White *tiaré* and orchids."

"Ma, she's going to be the prettiest bride on earth!" Abby exclaimed.

Ma smiled at Abby. "I do believe you're right. I wonder what Uncle Samuel will be wearing."

"Actually," Lani said, "Mahoi also brought a wrapped package for Samuel. It's soft, like material . . . so maybe it's something for him to wear in the wedding."

"Then," Abby reasoned, "we'll sail back to Matavai Bay and have the wedding on the ship so Duncan—as captain—can marry you two?"

"Yes. Afterward we'll go ashore and have a wedding picnic on the beach with Mahoi's family. It will be a small celebration but still nice. They insisted on doing most of the meal," Lani explained. "They have been so kind," she said, tears flooding her eyes, ". . . and it's everything I've ever dreamed of."

Ma leaned over and hugged Lani.

But Abby felt ashamed. Mahoi and Aimata had graciously given so much, yet they barely knew their new island guests. She, however, had known Luke for years. He was her best friend, but she hadn't been generous with him at all. *I've let little things build up and bother me about him,* she thought unhappily. *Then I judged him for losing that pearl, when I should have been gracious and loving toward him. I'm sorry, God. Please bring Luke home soon so I can tell him I'm sorry, too.*

That afternoon, however, Luke wasn't home yet when Abby had to rush from the harbor to the palace on her own. She'd promised to meet Rahiti by three o'clock so she could get in to see Jean-Paul.

She brought cinnamon rolls this time to give to Vatu. *I hope it sweetens his attitude,* she thought as she hiked across the palace grounds. She walked to the back of the building to meet Rahiti near the kitchen when she came upon the beautiful garden area she'd seen the first day, through the hall windows near the queen's quarters. Just as she was heading toward them to see the gardenia and bird-of-paradise up close, one of the double doors of the palace opened. Instinctively she dropped behind a tree and peered cautiously out.

A tall athletic man, wearing a straw hat pulled low, was slipping from the palace through the queen's quarters. Though dressed in Western clothes, Abby could see he was a Tahitian. He opened the front of his shirt and slipped a wrapped bundle into it. When he looked up, Abby inhaled in surprise. It was Tunui! What was he doing lurking around the queen's quarters again? He certainly acted suspicious the way he looked both ways, then hurried away.

As soon as he was well on his way toward the street, Abby left her hiding place and hurried toward the back of the palace. *What should I do? Should I tell Rahiti?* Her mind was in turmoil. *Tunui and Rahiti are friends, but with that rumor of a spy . . . oh, I wish Luke were here!*

No sooner did she arrive at the back steps than Rahiti came sauntering up, whistling happily. She hated to ruin his good mood, but she had to mention what she'd seen.

"When I was walking around the back of the palace," she said, pointing, "I saw a man coming out of the queen's quarters."

Rahiti's head came up sharply.

"It was Tunui," she said.

Rahiti relaxed. "He's a mysterious person," he said, "but I trust him."

"Okay," Abby said, hoping that Rahiti's trust was well placed. They walked quietly through the kitchen and into the long hall. Jean-Paul grinned when they arrived, and Rahiti motioned for Vatu to take a break. "I've got some chores to do," Rahiti told Vatu, "and Abby brought you a treat, so why don't you come with me and we can talk?" Vatu didn't ankle-cuff Jean-Paul this time, and Abby was glad. Perhaps Vatu was beginning to trust her with his prisoner.

Having a break from Vatu seemed to improve Jean-Paul's spirits, too. They chatted while Jean-Paul painted and taught. But when the two teens returned, Jean-Paul grew quiet. As Abby said good-bye, he bent over to kiss her hand. Although it was typical of the French, no one had ever done that to her before, and Abby blushed.

As she walked back to the harbor alone, she thanked God for this opportunity to learn from a real artist. Several times Jean-Paul had urged her to take his brush; then he'd coached her through a spot on his canvas. Abby was honored by his trust and eager to learn more. And she'd also been able to secretly start on Luke's birthday gift.

As she approached the dock where she'd left the rowboat, she saw Luke's familiar shape sitting on the edge of the dock, his blond-streaked hair gold in the sun. He was watching the ships in the bay and obviously waiting for her.

"Hi." Abby came up and sat alongside him, her legs swinging over the water, too.

"How was the painting lesson?" he asked, turning his green eyes on her.

"Great, thanks." Abby paused, taking a big breath as Luke's eyes met hers. "Oh, Luke, I'm sorry. I just haven't been very nice to you lately. I said that mean thing about you losing the pearl and, ah, I've been feeling bad about it ever since."

His eyes softened; then a smile lit his face. "It's all right, Abby. I forgive you," he said. "We all have bad days. . . ." He reached into his shirt pocket and pulled out a little brown-paper package, handing it to her. "But I appreciate you saying it."

"What's this?"

"Open it and see." He watched as Abby unfolded

the paper. The sunlight hit the contents instantly, turning it to molten silver and sea tones.

"Luke, it's your pearl!" Abby closed her eyes. "But I thought you'd lost it."

"I never said that. I only said it wasn't here. Actually," he said, one cheek dimpling, "I had Rahiti drop it off at the jeweler's for me. I wanted it put in a setting so you could hang it from your gold chain," he said. Abby touched the delicate gold filigree cross and chain he'd given her. She had always treasured the necklace because it had once belonged to Luke's mother.

"I should've known," she said, feeling her eyes moisten. "But I don't really deserve it . . ."

"'Course you do," he said, grinning. "Take off the chain, and I'll slip the pearl on it."

Abby undid the clasp and handed the necklace to Luke. He slid the pearl on the chain and gave it back to her.

"It will hang in front of the cross," he said, "but it will still look nice. That pearl's a beaut. Imagine pulling something that valuable out of a slimy old oyster!"

Clasping the chain around her neck again she touched the pearl's smooth surface and gazed at its dazzling, silver-blue depths.

"It's pretty valuable," Luke commented, "according to that jeweler anyway."

Abby threw her arms around him in a fierce hug. "It's one in a million. Just like you."

"Girls and their pearls," Luke said with a chuckle.

Chapter Nine

Over the next two days, the Kendalls and crew fell into a comfortable routine. Abby still went to the palace each afternoon to visit Jean-Paul and get painting lessons while Lani and Ma were busy with the wedding plans. Sarah took charge of keeping Sandy out of the way while the women worked long hours on the gorgeous wedding gown, now almost done. Abby had seen Lani in it, and she warned Uncle Samuel to get ready for a rare treat. Poor Uncle Samuel seemed more smitten than ever with his bride-to-be. His big gray eyes followed her around the deck in admiration. But Lani, so preoccupied with details, barely noticed.

While Abby helped out with chores in the mornings, the men and Luke busied themselves with stocking the ship for the return trip to Hawaii, fishing, or going on hunting forays inland. So far they'd come back empty-handed, but today Mahoi and Rahiti were able to get away from their work. They would take the Kendall crew inland to the best place to find wild boar. They might not be home until dusk, Luke had warned, so Abby headed for her afternoon painting lesson alone.

Jean-Paul was working on the second portrait, which was of the king's wife. He'd been teaching only a short while when Vatu returned from his break earlier than usual. Abby, however, was glad he had, because seconds later they heard someone coming down the hallway. The door was open to let the air flow through, so Abby jumped up in a panic. "Behind the bedstead," Jean-Paul said. Abby had no sooner thrown herself behind the side of the bed when the footsteps entered Jean-Paul's room.

"How much longer?" The harsh voice belonged to Chief Ono, Abby knew. She lay low, her heart beating wildly in her chest.

"Perhaps three or four days," Jean-Paul answered; then a stream of French broke from him, which seemed to enrage the chief.

"The queen returns sooner than that. You are dragging your feet! It must be finished now. I intend to present the portraits to her officially."

French words again erupted and Abby cringed. Jean-Paul was bound to make his captor angrier.

But Chief Ono didn't yell this time. He grew ominously quiet. His voice lowered. "If it is not finished by tomorrow, I will lash you with the whip. Then you will have something to complain about, you French swine."

Jean-Paul remained silent and unmoving until the footsteps receded. Abby lifted her head in time to see him shake his head. His face was mottled with red spots of anger. Suddenly he jumped up, towering over his paint jars. His arm crashed downward, sweeping three of them from the table. Glass crashed to the floor, spilling colors on the dry boards.

Abby hurried over. "Let me help you clean up the mess," she said, bending down on one knee.

"No," Jean-Paul said, "you might get cut." He reached quickly for a paint-stained shard but evidently didn't see a clear piece that jutted up between it and his hand. Instantly the painter cried out in anguish as the glittering glass sliced between his thumb and palm.

"Oh no!" Abby collected the cloth napkin from the basket she'd brought and quickly wrapped his hand in it. "Vatu, please get us some more clean cloths," she ordered. The youth hurried from the room, casting a glance over his shoulder at the cloth that was already red with blood.

"How stupid of me, *mon amie*. I am an idiot . . . and worse, I am without hope."

"Right now it does look hopeless," Abby admitted, "but your grandpa was right. God has a reason for everything. The Tahitian people, they're in a similar situation as you. The French have taken over their land, and they're miserable about it."

"Don't you think I know this?" Jean-Paul looked tortured by Abby's attempt at encouragement.

"But wait!" she said. "A Tahitian friend of mine

told me something that makes a lot of sense. She doesn't think about the situation anymore. She keeps her eyes on God and looks for things to thank Him for. She trusts He will somehow bring good out of the bad. Kind of like this pearl," Abby said, showing him her gift from Luke. Then she explained how the oyster had taken an irritating grain of sand that was making its life miserable and had coated it with mother-of-pearl in order to keep from feeling the pain.

Jean-Paul still looked glum. "I don't expect God to change things. I think He ez not so interested in my little problems . . . and Abby, I am *not* an oyster."

She smiled at his attempt at humor. "But when we coat our problems with prayer, Jean-Paul, our hurt softens."

Jean-Paul stared at her. "I only wish I had your faith, Abby."

Vatu returned at that moment. They finished picking up the glass with his help. Abby took away the blood-soaked cloth. Her sympathetic eyes met Jean-Paul's as she wrapped his palm in dry linens. "You must rest it now."

Jean-Paul's face darkened. "No, I must finish this and get free from here. That is when I will thank God." But when Jean-Paul tried to pick up his paintbrush to continue working, he cried out in pain and dropped the brush.

"Oh no," Abby said. "Chief Ono will have to

understand that you're injured and can't finish now."

But Vatu shook his head, his dark eyes hooded. "He will not change what he has ordered. That not be the way of a powerful *ari'i*—of a chief. Once a command be spoken, it not be taken back. Tomorrow if this painting not be done, Jean-Paul will be lashed with the whip."

Abby saw the look on Jean-Paul's face before he turned away. This was a crushing blow. Concern for Jean-Paul flooded Abby.

Somehow she just had to find a way to stop the cruel punishment that would surely come with tomorrow's sunrise.

Chapter Ten

Luke watched as Abby paced the foredeck of the *Kamana,* a light breeze riffling her hair. The sunset was just now turning the sky into layers of blushing gold that reminded Luke of yellow and pink plumeria blossoms. They were alone, the family belowdecks, and Luke was glad because Abby was in a snit.

"We can't just stand by and let Jean-Paul get whipped!" Outrage punctuated Abby's hand gestures. Her eyes snapped with fire. "I don't see how we can change the chief's order," she told him, "but there's no way that painting can be finished by tomorrow. He can't even hold a brush!"

Abby was right, of course, but Luke didn't feel as outraged as she. For one thing, he was tired after a long day of hiking and hunting. And there might be a way around it anyway. He rubbed his chin thoughtfully. "But you can."

"What?" She turned to face him, and the pale

pink light fell on her cinnamon curls, burnishing them to bronze.

"You can hold a brush. He's taught you to paint for four days already. You told me he's even trusted you with some strokes on his canvas. Well, he's got no choice but to trust you now."

"Luke, I can't possibly. I-I'm not an artist like him."

He could see her swallow nervously, which meant one thing. She was considering the possibility. "Abby, he could coach you through it. At any rate, if you care at all about him—and I know you do— then what choice do you have?"

Abby looked pale.

"You can do this, Abby. I know it," Luke said. "And I'll help sneak you into the palace—"

She turned to him, her face clearly nervous. Then she seemed to make a decision. Straightening her shoulders, she sighed. "I guess I've just got to act like an oyster."

"You mean make a big shiny pearl out of this bad situation?" he finished for her.

When she nodded, he continued, "We'll take the rowboat in tonight while the palace is asleep. By morning that portrait will be done, and you'll have saved the day." Luke grinned.

Abby returned his grin and then headed below-decks.

Once Abby's mind was made up, Luke knew she'd go forward with her characteristic spunk.

Even as he watched her head toward the hatch, he saw her step more lightly, as if a burden had lifted.

Luke glanced at the sky. The colors had changed, deepening to the purples of the Tahitian orchids he'd so recently seen. He sat at the bow of the bobbing schooner and took out the wood he was whittling and his pocketknife. He had a while to wait, and he felt reflective as he gazed heavenward. The first star was out, hanging in the fathomless blue. He often took a moment to watch the sunset and the first star rising. But tonight its beauty captured him.

He thought back to how it'd been before he'd become a Christian in California. Then the night sky had only brought a lonely pain to his heart. *Ma and Pa were dead and gone,* he remembered, *and it felt like there was an ocean of sky between us. And no way to span the distance.* How cold the starlight had seemed when he'd been aching for his ma's warm arms.

But tonight Luke didn't feel lonely. The dark sky no longer looked vast and comfortless. *I've got a way to span that distance now. I've got the Lord, and with Him all the love and peace anyone could want. He's taken that painful ache and coated it with His love for me.*

Gentle swells lapped the *Kamana*'s hull. The air was soft. From here, Papeete seemed to be coming alive as oil lamps were just now being lit. Luke glanced heavenward again. *All that darkness,* he thought, *but God will never let the stars go out.*

Two hours later, when everyone else was asleep,
Luke tied the rowboat to the dock and helped Abby
out. They hurried toward Papeete's main street and
walked as fast as Abby could go. Hiking along
Boulevard Pomare, Abby commented, "It looks
different at night."

She was right, Luke realized. Although a few
families strolled the boulevard, music from water-
front saloons wafted on the pleasant breeze, calling
to sailors who were on shore leave. Drinking places
were doing a brisk business. Here and there pairs of
French soldiers, sabers clanking on their hips,
walked the streets, apparently keeping their eyes
open for troublemakers.

Abby and Luke kept walking south, with
streetlamps and hotels lighting their way as they
headed toward the palace. The constant sound of
waves and the scent of the sea traveled with them.

Once they reached the palace grounds, they cut
around to the back, staying in the shadows of swaying palms and giant ferns. "Look," Abby whispered,
"there's a guard at Jean-Paul's window."

Luke could tell the guard was a muscular full-
grown man. By the light of the moon, Luke caught
a glimpse of steel on the ground—an unsheathed
sword lay at his feet. He was sitting underneath the
open window and his head turned this way and

that, which told Luke he was alert. With the sea wind, the curtains wafted in and out of the window just above his head.

"Come on," Luke urged, steering Abby quietly behind trees toward the kitchen's back door.

By now it was about 10 o'clock. They both hoped the kitchen help would be in bed, because if anyone should see them, it would be hard to come up with an explanation for entering the palace without Rahiti accompanying them.

Luckily the guard at Jean-Paul's window was not in a position to see the kitchen entrance. Luke motioned for Abby to wait while he checked to see if the way was clear. "What if the door's locked?" Abby whispered, a possibility Luke was only now considering.

"We'll cross that bridge when we come to it," he said. Then he silently hurried toward the back door. It creaked loudly as he opened it; then he slipped in. Two minutes later he exited and stood on the porch, motioning for Abby to join him.

As she did, he whispered, "The coast is clear. Should be smooth sailing to Jean-Paul."

They moved through the dark kitchen as quietly as possible, listening for footsteps but hearing only the regulator clock ticking in the corner. Soon they were in the hallway, and Luke lit a match so they could locate the right door and the black key.

Abby turned it in the lock, and they quickly entered the room.

Jean-Paul instantly sat up in bed. "Who's there?" he called out softly.

Luke pulled Abby down to a crouch behind the table. He waited a moment to see if the guard had been alerted, but nothing moved outside.

Crawling toward Jean-Paul, Luke whispered, "It's us, Jean-Paul—Abby and Luke."

Abby followed.

When they reached him, Jean-Paul reached out his uninjured hand. "My friends," he said, touching their heads. His white teeth flashed in a smile.

"We're here to help you finish the painting," Abby said hopefully.

His face scrunched into a scowl as he considered the idea. Then he leaned forward. "We will shut the drapes quietly, *mon amie;* then I shall light a candle. But we will have to be ever so silent—for the guard is on duty."

Luke nodded. "We've seen him outside."

Jean-Paul got up and crept to the window, silently sliding the drapes shut. Luke hoped the wind wouldn't whip up. If it did, it would reveal candle-light, and the guard might decide to come investigate. Should he part the curtains, they'd surely be caught!

Chapter Eleven

Abby nerously rolled up the sleeves on her blouse and donned a painter's smock. Jean-Paul smoothed his moustache and nodded at her to pick up the brush. By the light of the candle, he was now ready to help her begin.

Luke sat under the window, listening for any movement of the guard as the two painters began their work. "I've already done most of it, so it will be much easier, *oui?*" Jean-Paul said quietly.

Abby examined the painting and was glad to see that much of it was already done. There was just a portion of the face and half of the background left to do.

But still she was nervous. Yet through the long night Jean-Paul remained patient and kind, directing and encouraging her as the first hour blended into two, then three. "You see, the lower lip ez in shadow, *oui?*" They began to fall into a rhythm, with Jean-Paul whispering and pointing at the canvas, Abby nodding, then dipping the brush into a color and applying it. Sometime in the midst of their work, Abby began to relax and actually enjoy painting. She was encouraged by his frequent, *"Oui!"* which told her she was doing well.

"And the eyes, *mon amie,* they always have a highlight in them. This is the white dot you see there." Abby saw exactly what he meant, and she dipped the thinnest brush into white paint as Jean-Paul pointed to the spot on the canvas.

"Perfect," he murmured. Abby glanced over to see if Luke had heard, but he was fast asleep under the window. He'd slipped from a sitting position and had fallen over onto his side. Still his mouth gaped open and a soft snore issued forth. She grinned and motioned at Jean-Paul to look. The artist, forgetting himself, chuckled loudly.

Abby's eyes widened in fear. *The guard!* There was a sudden noise outside, and Abby ducked behind Jean-Paul's chair. He instantly leaned over and blew out the candle, but would the guard see them anyway?

The drapes lifted! Silhouetted against the sinking moon, the guard's head and beefy shoulders appeared. Luke lay right under his nose, but maybe the guard would only look into the room, not directly under the window. Abby closed her eyes tightly, afraid to look again. She held very still.

There was a snort and another scuffle outside, and she couldn't help but open her eyes. The drapes were back in place, the guard gone.

Jean-Paul put a hand on her shoulder. "Let's take

a little break," he whispered. "We'll start up again soon, but perhaps the guard will go to sleep like our friend Luke."

They both tiptoed over to the door area, far from the window, and sat leaning against a wall. "So, tell me all about your family, Abby," Jean-Paul coaxed. "I want to hear how you came to be in Tahiti."

Abby launched into the story of how her Uncle Samuel had gotten sick in Hawaii and the whole family had sailed from California to help him. "Luke was my best friend and an orphan," she explained. "But his Aunt Dagmar wouldn't let him come with us, so he stowed away."

Jean-Paul grinned. "That ez dedication. But now that I know you, I can see why he did it."

She smiled. "Eventually Luke and I ended up back in California, where Duncan bought the ship we're on. By the time he brought us back to Hawaii, my uncle had lost his ranch. So we joined up with Duncan as his trading partners. We're here in Tahiti so Lani and Uncle Samuel can get married."

"I imagine your Uncle Samuel ez a lucky man," the artist said.

"Oh yes. Lani is one of the most wonderful women in the world and beautiful, too."

Jean-Paul grew quiet. When he next spoke, his voice was serious and contemplative. "There ez only one thing more wonderful than love to a French-man. And that ez freedom. I cannot tell you how much I long to be free—to walk out of this little room. Have you ever lost your freedom, Abby?"

Abby swallowed hard at the memory that surfaced. "Once Luke and I were captured by a pirate named Jackal. He was going to sell us as slaves in China."

Jean-Paul's eyebrows rose with interest. "*Mon amie!* How did you escape this Jackal?"

"I, ah, whacked him on the head with a big pepper shaker." Abby's eyes glistened at the memory. "And then I took his treasure map." She wondered if Jean-Paul would think she was awful for doing that. Of course, the treasure had turned out to be Duncan's anyway.

But Jean-Paul was holding his sides, trying not to laugh out loud. He finally wiped his eyes and patted her on the cheek with his good hand. "This ez the best moment I have had in many days, *mon amie.* I will remember to stay away from you and ze pepper shaker."

Abby grinned. "Actually, you could use one right now, huh?"

"*Oui,*" he said, sobering. "The palace, it ez a place of intrigue—but not just for me. Two nights ago I hear voices under my window. One is a woman, another a man—perhaps the guard who ez always out there. They are speaking of rebellion against the French."

"I bet they were," Abby said. "My friend told me some of the Tahitians hate the French now."

"*Oui,* but this was not just about the French. I

heard them say something about overthrowing the queen. . . ." Jean-Paul drew closer to her, his face intense. "What I heard, Abby, it made the hair on my neck stand up. I do not know this queen, but it made me sad for her. They are plotting to take over her throne so they can raise up a rebellion and fight the French."

"They must be Tahitian rebels," Abby said, clearly upset now.

"*Oui.* They think if they remove the queen, the islanders will try one last time to fight the French and win their freedom."

"Oh, how terrible. I've heard there aren't many Tahitian men left to fight. . . ." Abby recalled the many French soldiers and that man-of-war in the harbor. When she closed her eyes for a moment, a vision popped into her head. She saw Tunui sneaking out of the queen's quarters, with the bundle under his shirt. Could he be in on this plan of rebellion?

"*Oui,* it ez bad. But what can we do?" Jean-Paul sighed heavily. "We do not know who to trust with this information. And the queen, she is not here anyway."

"I will pray," Abby whispered. Feeling an urgency about it, she bowed her head and silently poured out her concerns to God. And she would remember to tell Rahiti as soon as she saw him. When she raised her head she saw that Jean-Paul had lit the candle once again. He held out the palette and brush for her.

The sun was just starting to lighten the horizon when Abby and Jean-Paul finished their work. Abby bent down and gently shook Luke awake. He rubbed his eyes and almost yawned, but Abby covered his mouth. "Shhh!"

Luke sat up and grinned. He sauntered over to see the final result and sighed. "Amazing," he said with a shake of his head. "You two have done it!"

"Oui." Jean-Paul nodded and smiled warmly. "She has the makings of a fine artist."

Abby blushed to her roots. "I have a great teacher." But her heart surged with satisfaction. They had created a portrait of a woman who looked real.

"Well, this little party has to come to an end so we can get out before we're caught," Luke said. "You ready, Abby?"

Abby was just starting to take off the smock when the door burst open. The outside guard filled the doorway ominously, then entered the room with his sword drawn. Abby saw several more guards waiting in the hall. Through their midst strode a muscle-bound older man with silver in his hair. He stalked powerfully into the room. Holding the whip in his right hand, he smacked it rythmically into his left palm. He wore only a red print *pareu* and a shell necklace around his massive neck. His broad face looked grim in the gray light.

"Chief Ono," Jean-Paul said with a slight inclination of his head, "the painting ez done."

The muscled Tahitian strode over to the canvas with narrowing eyes, then stood back to view the finished painting. Abby could see he approved of the portrait, but when he turned back to Jean-Paul he looked displeased. "You avoid your whipping this time," he said gruffly.

Then he cast shrewd eyes on Abby and Luke, who were silently taking in the scene. "What are you doing here?" he asked harshly. The whip handle beat into his palm.

"We, ah, came to visit," Luke said nervously.

But the guard stepped forward, his chin jutting out, his dark eyes honing in on Abby. "I saw what they were doing. That one," he said, pointing to her, "helped him all night. She used the brush most of the time."

Abby wanted to shrink into the floor. How had the guard seen them? Had he peeked through the curtain when they hadn't noticed? She swallowed hard.

"Is this true?" Chief Ono demanded, his face hawklike and intense.

She opened her mouth but could think of nothing to say. She closed her mouth and turned desperate eyes on Jean-Paul.

Chief Ono's hooded eyes went to Jean-Paul and took in the bandaged hand. Abby could see him assessing the situation.

Suddenly the Tahitian pointed a menacing finger at Abby. "If you are so good at painting, then you shall stay here and help the Frenchman paint the next two portraits!"

"What?" Luke said, stepping forward. "You can't do that!"

"Next portraits?" Jean-Paul yelled. "I have finished as we agreed. Two portraits ez all. I am a free man now!" Abby sensed Jean-Paul's mounting panic. She felt it growing in herself as well. She couldn't stay here. Ma and Pa would be frantic!

But Chief Ono seemed unaffected by their desperate words. He smiled calmly, maliciously. He held the whip perfectly still, poised above his open palm. "You will be free," he said softly, "when I order it. Not before." Turning to the guard, he commanded, "Take the girl and put her in the women's servant quarters. Lock her in until later in the day, when she will come back to work. I am not unreasonable. She may rest since she has been up all night."

"You can't do that!" Luke retorted, his voice high-pitched. He moved to place himself between the guard and Abby.

But Abby instantly sensed that Luke was close to getting arrested, too. If that happened she wouldn't be able to get a message to her parents. She needed Luke free. She needed him to help her escape—somehow!

She put a hand on his arm and pulled him back. "No, Luke, it's okay." Her voice remained steady and calm. Her eyes bored into his, begging him to understand. "Go tell Ma and Pa what's happened. I'll be okay. I'm sure this won't be for long . . ." Her eyes pleaded with him to understand. For a moment he wavered, then she saw understanding in his green eyes.

Luke took a deep breath, brushing one hand through his short hair. She could see him trying desperately to get a grip on himself as he turned. "I'll tell them, and I'll be back to visit you two. . . . If it's all right with the chief."

The Tahitian's scowl softened a bit as Luke's tone became submissive. "If the girl does as she's told, you may visit tomorrow." With that, he marched from the room. The guard waited until Luke headed through the doorway before he exited with Abby in tow.

"Good-bye, Jean-Paul. I–I'll see you later," Abby called.

Jean-Paul's eyes were stony flint until he turned to Abby. Then she watched them flood with compassion. "I am so sorry," he said softly.

"It'll be okay," she promised. "Remember the oyster."

As brave as she planned to be, it didn't take long for such thoughts to get buried under a tidal wave of fear. Several guards surrounded Luke and marched him away from Abby's sight, and her heart clenched into a painful knot.

Alone! she thought, as she was marched down an

unknown hallway. *Even when we were taken captive by Jackal, Luke was with me. But now I'm alone in the palace with a crazy, power-hungry chief. I'm going to be locked up like a criminal.*

As one guard shoved her down another hallway toward the women's quarters, all Abby could think of was Jean-Paul's last tortured look. The words he'd so recently spoken came back to haunt her: "There ez only one thing more wonderful than love to a Frenchman. And that ez freedom."

She was beginning to understand those feelings.

Chapter Twelve

Luke raced back to the harbor and jumped into the rowboat, plowing through the low, easy swells with vigor. *What are we going to do?* he thought. *This is all my fault. It was my idea to go to the palace! Oh, Lord, please help us figure out what to do. Please help Abby's ma and pa to . . . to not panic.*

But Luke was close to panic himself. All he could think about was Abby being carted off by that big, beefy guard.

As soon as Luke rowed close to the *Kamana,* he called out to Duncan, who sat on the deck of the bobbing schooner with his morning mug of coffee. Duncan set down the mug and hurried to the rope ladder. As Luke tied off the boat at the ladder, Duncan leaned over. "What are ye doing out this early, lad?"

Luke cast a glance at him, then raced up the ladder, his heart pounding fiercely. "We've got a problem, Duncan. And I'm glad I've run into you first." The two had become fast friends in the last

10 months—it had even gone beyond friendship, almost to a father-son relationship. Luke was glad to have the quick-witted Scotsman on his side.

"Maybe ye'd best sit down to do yer explaining," Duncan suggested, one dark eyebrow raised quizzically. He steered him amidships to the bulkhead. "Now what's eatin' ye?"

Luke heaved a sigh. "It's all my fault. I suggested Abby go help Jean-Paul finish his painting at the palace last night—seeing as how the chief was planning on lashing him if it wasn't finished by morning, and he'd cut himself so badly."

Duncan put up a hand. "Whoa, son. Ye'd best start at the beginning and slow down."

Luke wiped the perspiration off his forehead and started again. Halfway through, Duncan began to look concerned. By the end of the tale, he'd leapt up and was pacing the deck. "By the horn spoons!" he shouted. "Who does this chief think he is, takin' an innocent girl hostage? Thomas and I will be visitin' him before he's had time for breakfast, I'm thinkin'."

Luke hadn't expected this from Duncan. He'd expected a calm plan to be laid out, something that was sure to work for Abby. But Duncan was outraged, and at that moment—to Luke's mortification—he spied Mr. Kendall's head coming up the hatch.

Abby's pa grinned at the two of them. "How'd you sleep, Luke?" he asked lightheartedly. Then, when Luke remained silent, Mr. Kendall looked more closely at him. "You're looking green around the gills, Luke."

"Thomas," Duncan ordered, "sit down. There's trouble afoot, and I'm afraid it involves Abby."

Mr. Kendall sat, his eyes quickly roaming the deck. Luke heaved another sigh and nervously began explaining. By the end of it Abby's pa was shaking his head and pacing the deck right behind Duncan.

"Luke, would you get me some coffee?" he asked. "Then we're off to get my daughter." As Luke descended the hatch he could hear Abby's pa and Duncan making plans. A minute later Luke was back on deck with the coffee.

Mr. Kendall drank the hot brew in three quick gulps and handed the empty mug back to Luke. "Don't discuss this with Abby's ma unless she asks for Abby, do you hear?"

"Yes, sir. But can't I come with you?"

"No. Duncan and I need to go. And don't worry—we'll bring Abby back."

Luke had never seen Abby's pa look as dead serious as he did climbing down the rope ladder to the waiting rowboat. Not another word passed between them as they departed, but to Luke's amazement, he spied Duncan tucking his pistol in the waistband at the back of his pants, under his vest.

Luke watched them row to shore, climb out, and take off at a brisk pace. Then he lost them among the trees and the morning foot traffic. He sat down and began to whittle, praying that Abby's ma would sleep unusually late this morning.

"Morning, Luke," Mrs. Kendall said as her head popped up from the hatch and she strolled toward him. "It's a lovely morning, don't you think?"

"Jehoshaphat," Luke whispered under his breath. He knew the story by heart but hoped she wouldn't ask about Abby so he wouldn't have to tell it again—especially not to Abby's tenderhearted ma.

But his hope was short-lived, for that was the very next question she asked.

An hour later Sarah was the first to sight the men rowing back to the *Kamana*. "Abby's not with them, Ma!" she yelled.

As Mrs. Kendall and Sarah rushed to the railing to greet the men, Luke searched their faces for any hint of what had transpired. They looked grim, and his heart sank.

Mr. Kendall and Duncan hadn't even finished climbing the rope ladder before Abby's ma burst out, "What happened, Thomas?" She'd been a bundle of nerves ever since Luke had explained why Abby was missing over an hour ago.

Abby's pa lumbered up the ladder with Duncan at his heels and motioned for everyone to sit down amidships. "We got to the palace, expecting this

Chief Ono to understand we need our daughter back, but the scoundrel didn't even come to see us."

Duncan interjected, "He sent 20 arrrmed guards, however." He appeared aggravated and twirled his handlebar moustache absently.

"Armed guards!" Mrs. Kendall shrieked. "When's he letting Abby go? Is she safe? Did you see her, Thomas?"

"We ran into a young man who works there just before we were pushed out the door," Mr. Kendall explained. "Vatu is his name. He told us that Abby is fine but will be held indefinitely until some portraits are finished. Just before those guards showed up to escort us off the grounds, he whispered that Luke should try visiting her tomorrow. He thought Chief Ono would allow it."

Luke stood up. "Yes, that's what he told me, too. I'll go first thing tomorrow."

"There's no way Duncan and I are going to be allowed in to visit her," Abby's pa said dejectedly. "We created too much of a ruckus today."

Duncan cleared his throat. "We have to plan her escape right away, so Luke can explain it to her tomorrow."

"An escape? You mean we'll be leaving Tahiti?" Sarah asked, her blue eyes widening with interest.

"Good idea, Sarah," Mr. Kendall said. "If it looks like we're leaving, the chief might let down his guard and not watch her so closely. That could make it easier to get her out. He's so heartless he'd easily believe we're leaving her behind."

"If the *Kamana* actually sailed away," Luke said, "there is a way Abby could meet us somewhere else."

Everyone turned to Luke, their faces full of questions.

"Jean-Paul has a flying balloon stashed somewhere outside Papeete," Luke said excitedly. "He told Abby it just needs to be set up, and then he can fly away. I could stay and create a diversion after the *Kamana* sails away. Then I could help Abby and Jean-Paul escape. The three of us could get to the balloon and sail it across the channel there," Luke said, pointing toward the distant island, "to Mooréa."

Everyone was so quiet that the noise of the swells slapping the hull suddenly sounded loud. "It could worrrk," Duncan said finally.

"I think so, too," Abby's pa agreed. "But why so far? Why not rendezvous in Matavai Bay? It's closer, and then we could be on our way much sooner."

"Jean-Paul said it takes a while for the balloon to elevate, then come down again. Matavai Bay is awfully close. It would just have gotten off the ground and then it would have to lower again. A man on a swift horse could probably keep up with you. But if you sail the schooner to a bay on Mooréa Island during the afternoon, we could fly to the island more quickly than anyone could follow. Jean-Paul could land us there; then he'd be free to sail on his way—and we could be on our way."

"I don't like the idea of her . . . flying in one of those contraptions," Abby's ma said nervously. "Are they safe?"

"Abby gets all the adventures," Sarah said with a frown. "Why couldn't I be taken hostage and get to escape in a flying machine?"

"What choice do we have, Charlotte?" Abby's pa asked, combing one big hand through his sandy hair.

Luke gazed around the group. Everyone sat still, their faces deeply concerned by the serious turn of events.

Then Mrs. Kendall cried out, "Oh no! If we have to leave Tahiti like this, Lani and Samuel won't get their wedding!"

Luke put his head in his hands. Just 12 hours ago peace had flooded his heart. He had been sure life was going to work out perfectly. Now Abby was a prisoner, her parents were all upset, and Lani wouldn't get her big wedding.

How have I managed to ruin it for everybody with one lousy idea? he thought.

And worse, what if our plan doesn't work?

Chapter Thirteen

Abby was tired of being pushed from behind by a rude guard. He opened a door and directed her in with a beefy hand on her back. In a glance Abby saw she was alone in the room. Against each of the four walls was a rope bed, with a lightweight quilt over it. A washstand and one large dresser stood near the window.

As soon as the door shut with a bang, a lock turned and then there was only silence. Abby walked to the window. She was on the west side of the palace, for she could see the distant harbor from here. There, just off to her right, was the *Kamana*. The window was open, the white eyelet curtains blowing softly in the early morning wind. She could just climb through and be on her way. Back to Ma, Pa, and Luke! Hope speared through her.

Seconds later she heard footsteps and saw her rude guard outside. He was approaching her window. She drew back so he wouldn't see her, but he did stop and sit beneath the window. Abby's heart plummeted. Suddenly she felt exhausted.

After being up all night, she was too tired to fight it anymore.

Abby sank wearily onto the bed by the door. The straw pallet rustled as she turned over, away from the window light. She wanted to go home, but her head ached from painting all night.

I'm just too tired to figure out what to do, she thought with a sigh. *After a short nap, I'll think better. Then I'll figure it out.*

Closing her eyes, Abby snuggled under the quilt and fell into a deep, deep sleep.

The sound of water splashing merged with Abby's dream of swimming in the sea, where a giant snake lunged at her from the dark depths. Her eyes flew open, taking in the shadowed room, but her head felt thick and sluggish. *Where am I?*

Water still splashed.

Abby sat up quickly and glanced toward the window. The drapes had been shut, and a woman stood with her back to Abby. She was bending over the washbasin, dipping her hands into the water, then scrubbing her face. A long dark braid trailed down her back, and she wore a typical mission dress of white and midnight blue. Abby watched as she reached blindly for the towel and dried her face.

When she turned around, Abby saw it was the same parlor maid she and Luke had seen the first day they'd come to the palace with Rahiti. "Is this your room?" Abby asked.

The young woman's eyes narrowed. "Yes. You be sharing it with me for a while."

A chill ran up Abby's neck. The way the woman had spoken made Abby feel as though she knew everything and had been a part of her imprisonment. "What's your name?" Abby asked.

"I am called Reva." She smoothed her braid at her temples. "And you are Abby."

For some reason it was unnerving that the woman already knew her name. "Do you know how long I'll be here?"

"Until you finish what Chief Ono says to do," she said, turning back to hang up the towel. "Don't worry. He is wonderful man. I should know—he is distant relative."

Abby kept quiet as Reva went to the dresser, rearranged its contents, and took out a white silk shawl, draping it over her shoulders.

"I will be gone for dinner," Reva said, as she shoved the dresser drawer shut. "Vatu be here soon to take you to your work."

"Will I get dinner soon?" Abby asked. She'd missed both breakfast and lunch, and now her stomach grumbled unhappily.

"How should I know? I not your nursemaid. Ask Vatu." With that Reva spun on her heel and left, slamming the door.

"Welcome to the palace," Abby said softly to

herself. The quiet of the room unsettled her. She walked to the window, hoping against hope that there would be no guard and she could slip away. But he was still there. Even if he was asleep, as he appeared to be, she would have to step on his shoulder to get down. And that would surely wake him.

Abby bit her lip anxiously and leaned her elbows on the windowsill. Her eyes sought out the *Kamana,* still at anchor in the quiet harbor. *They're still there, and they won't leave until I am on board with them.*

The thought was immensely comforting. She imagined Sarah on deck, playing with Sandy. Luke whittling at the bow, his favorite spot, and Ma stirring a cook pot that wafted the succulent smells of gravy and chipped beef. Pa would be opening up the big Bible on the kitchen table, deciding on a passage to read after dinner, while Duncan and Uncle Samuel might be checking the anchor line. No doubt Lani would be trying on her finished wedding gown in front of the small oval mirror in Ma's cabin.

The wedding! Abby gasped as she realized they couldn't have the wedding until she was released! They would wait for her, wouldn't they? Oh, what a fine mess things had become. Now Lani's perfectly planned wedding would have to be postponed. If only Rahiti found out she was here, he might be able to do something to help.

A knock sounded loudly on the door. A muffled

voice called, and then the door burst open. Vatu
sauntered into the room. "Come on," he said pleas-
antly. "Chief Ono says you and Jean-Paul start a
new painting. The queen returns in two days, and
he wants this one done."

"Vatu, have you seen Rahiti today?" Abby asked
as they walked down the long hallway.

"No," Vatu hissed, "and don't go asking me
again. If I tell him you are here, he get in trouble
with Chief Ono. Is that what you want?"

"No." Abby's stomach growled loudly again.
"Could I have some dinner in Jean-Paul's room?"

"Hungry, eh? When the last time you ate?"

"Dinner last night."

"Guess we need feed you if we want you work,"
Vatu said. "I lock you in. Then find some food for
you from cooks."

By now they'd reached Jean-Paul's door, which
Vatu unlocked. Abby was glad to enter and see
Jean-Paul's friendly smiling face. Then the door
lock clicked again.

Abby and Jean-Paul studied a pencil sketch of a
young teen girl who sat regal and proud. The girl,
probably about Abby's age, wore an elegant dark
silk dress with a feathered cape about her shoulders.
There was a jeweled choker at her throat and a
diamond- and pearl-studded crown in the thick

dark hair piled on her head. "She must be a young Tahitian princess," Abby said.

And yet, for some reason, the young girl looked familiar.

Her thoughts were interrupted when Vatu entered, carrying a plate of rice and vegetables. Abby ate quickly as Jean-Paul began to outline the shape of the princess's head and shoulders with his left hand. He slowly sketched in the eyes and nose with faint pencil lines but quickly grew frustrated with his clumsiness. He gingerly switched the pencil to his right hand to continue.

When Abby saw him wince with pain and drop the pencil, she insisted on changing his bandage, calling for Vatu to bring more clean cloths.

As soon as he returned with the items, Vatu left and she unfastened the bandage. The cut was raw and red but beginning to heal. "I'm sorry," she said, knowing it would hurt. Then she poured a liberal amount of water over it, washing it thoroughly. Jean-Paul's eyes smarted with tears, but he kept silent.

Abby tenderly rewrapped his injury. He sighed when it was over. "*Merci,*" he said.

"You must heal quickly," Abby whispered so the guard at the window would not hear, "because I'm sure my parents are forming a plan right now to get us out of here."

Jean-Paul swiped at his moustache nervously. "You think so?" he asked hopefully.

"Of course! They won't leave without me, and when I leave, you can also."

Abby turned back to the black-and-white pencil sketch of the girl. Again, something struck her as familiar. Who was this young girl? She shook the question from her mind as Jean-Paul told her, "Take notice of the distance of the mouth from the bottom of the chin, and start there." Abby leaned forward, realizing she could estimate the relationship of one feature to the next to get to her goal—sort of like hopping from stone to stone over a creek.

Taking her time, she softly drew in the girl's mouth, hair, crown, and choker with Jean-Paul's coaching. After a long while, he was content and urged her to begin painting.

Two hours later, Abby's guard returned for her. Now that she had left the friendly face of Jean-Paul, she dreaded facing the night alone in a strange place. When she got to her room, the guard left the oil lamp he'd been carrying. "Thank you," Abby said, meaning it. She didn't want to be alone in the dark. As he turned to leave, she asked, "What's your name?"

"Teva," he said shortly.

"That's a lot like Reva's name," Abby said, speaking of the parlor maid who shared the room.

"She my sister," Teva explained. "We get our jobs at same time from Chief Ono."

Abby only nodded as he turned and left. *If they got their jobs from Chief Ono, who's unfairly imprisoned me and Jean-Paul, I can't trust them.* She sighed and sneaked to the window, parting the curtains. A guard was already posted, one she'd never seen before. He glanced up at her, and she pulled back uneasily.

The washbasin had been emptied, so Abby poured fresh water from the pitcher into it and washed. Then she crawled onto the same bed. An aching loneliness wrapped around her. She thought about Sarah and Luke, possibly up late talking about her. *The whole family might be sitting on deck, gazing at the stars, or planning what to do next. But one thing's certain. At the end of their planning, they'll be praying for me.*

Ma's probably praying for my safety right now. At the thought of her mother's compassion, tears sprang to Abby's eyes. As she wiped them away, the door opened. Reva walked in, her face flushed with excitement.

But as soon as she saw Abby, she glanced at her dresser. "Did you go through my things?" she asked in a harsh tone.

"Of course not." Abby sat up and scowled.

But that's when Abby noticed it—a little piece of blue velvet had gotten caught in the drawer, forcing it to stay partially open when Reva had closed it so abruptly earlier.

"Oh," Reva said, bumping the drawer shut with

her hip and looking nervous. For the next few minutes she ignored Abby as she slipped into a nightdress and trimmed the lantern.

"Good night," Abby said softly into the dark. But the parlor maid only turned her back and slipped into sleep quickly.

Abby's sense of isolation deepened, and sleep took a long time coming.

Chapter Fourteen

The next morning Abby and Jean-Paul had been working for two hours when the door to Jean-Paul's room opened.

"Hi!" a voice called cheerfully before Abby could look up.

"Luke!" Abby raced over and threw her arms around his neck. "How did you get in?"

"Vatu thought it'd be okay—but he didn't ask Chief Ono, which was nice of him." When Luke grinned, Abby thought his dimple had never looked more welcome. The loneliness of the night before lifted. Suddenly the whole day seemed brighter.

Luke held up a cloth-covered basket. Abby grinned. "Ma's biscuits?"

"With mango jam," Luke said, setting it on the table. Jean-Paul pulled up a chair for Luke as he set out the large napkin and placed the jar of jam, a butter knife, and warm biscuits before them. Then, bowing his head, he prayed. "Thank You, Lord, for this good food, for how You care about our needs.

Thanks for the good ideas You've given us. Please bless our work and actions. Amen."

Abby opened her eyes. Luke winked at her.

"You've got a plan!" she whispered.

When he nodded, she urged him to tell. Luke kept his voice low. "Your pa and Duncan came here yesterday morning. Chief Ono sent them off, but they were followed. The chief's spying on our activities, Abby. We're sure of it."

Jean-Paul snorted with disgust. "The swine!"

"What's the plan, Luke?" Abby asked, glancing uneasily at the window where the guard was.

"We're gonna sail away, making it look like we've left you behind so they'll relax their guard."

Abby gripped Luke's arm in panic. "You can't sail away without me!" she whispered fiercely.

"They're going to sail away without me, too, Abby. You don't think I'd leave you, do you?"

She released his arm and sat back. Jean-Paul grinned at the two of them while heaping jam on a warm biscuit. He took a bite, sighed with pleasure, and announced, "I must meet this mother of yours, Abby."

This encouraged Abby to dig in, too, while Luke continued to tell them about the plan. "Okay, you both must continue working hard so they suspect nothing. Then tonight I'll be back with a plan up my sleeve. I'll get the outside guard to leave his post. When he does, we'll be gone."

"But, Luke, I might be in my sleeping quarters

and you don't know where that is," Abby said. "It's on the west side of the palace, because I can see the harbor from my window. And there's always a guard outside my window, too."

Luke crossed his arms and thought a moment. "I'll have to do something that's big enough to get everyone's attention. Somehow."

"Okay, let's say we figure that out. What next?" she asked.

Luke glanced at Jean-Paul. "We race to your captain's home and get your balloon in the air."

Jean-Paul stopped chewing. "It will take time to set it up, Luke. And if we are being followed, this plan will not work."

"You both must stuff pillows under your blankets so it looks like you're still asleep. That will give us more time," Luke said confidently.

"Where do we meet up with Ma and Pa?" Abby asked. She wasn't sure this plan was going to work either.

"On Mooréa," Luke said, as if this was as easy as pie. He turned to Jean-Paul. "Abby's ma wants me to ask you if that flying machine is safe and if you can steer it to Mooréa."

Jean-Paul wiped a crumb off his moustache. "*Oui*, it is safe as long as I've put it together properly. And *oui*, I can steer it . . . sort of."

Abby put her head in her hands and moaned.

Luke jumped up and paced, stopping in front of her. "If you have a better idea, let's hear it!"

She didn't. Jean-Paul also shook his head in defeat.

"Then it's a go," Luke said. "We're leaving tonight."

"But, Luke," Abby said, "what are you going to do to distract the guards—two of them on different sides of the palace?"

Luke sat down wearily in a chair and gazed at his feet. "I don't have a clue."

Abby and Jean-Paul worked together until early evening, when her guard came to get her. As she entered her room, she was surprised to see Reva dressing up to go out again. Though Abby was dying to rush to the window and see if the *Kamana* had already sailed, she had to wait until Reva left. The young woman seemed eager to get away from the palace, Abby thought. "Meeting someone special?" Abby asked, trying to be friendly.

Reva seemed to notice her for the first time. "It's not like that, but it is someone important," she said crisply. Then she gave her long braid a pat, glanced in the mirror a last time, and headed toward the door.

She'd just left when the door opened and Vatu arrived with Abby's dinner. The roasted chicken and yams smelled delicious. Abby thanked him as he left, turning the key in the lock behind him.

With the door locked, Abby would be warned if anyone was coming in. She hurried to the window and cautiously peered through the curtains. She could see much of the harbor from here. She searched for the spot the *Kamana* had been anchored. It wasn't there!

They had left her.

Abby searched the bay and saw in the far distance a schooner heading out to sea under full sail. *It could be them,* she thought with a sinking heart. The muscles along her shoulders tensed. She knew her parents were only fulfilling the plan, but still her heart wrenched with an aching loneliness. She couldn't see any good purpose coming from this whole mess.

Abby wandered back to her bed, crawled onto it, and curled up with her head on the pillow. She shut her eyes and breathed deeply, trying to relax the tension in her neck. Her mind drifted to other moments from the past, moments when it had looked as if evil would win.

Zai Ching, the pirate king, holding a knife to Ma's throat . . . Jackal tying Luke, Duncan, and Kini to the banyan tree . . . me and Luke waiting in the dark on Lanai in those awful pits—waiting for something very bad to happen while the drumbeats came closer.

Yet God had intervened.

You've always been with me, dear Lord.

Abby's neck relaxed, loosening the knots in her shoulders. Peace enveloped her, like a warm quilt tucked around her. And then she heard a soft voice speaking with both authority and compassion.

BE STILL, AND KNOW THAT I AM GOD.

Chapter Fifteen

Hours had passed.

Abby had eaten part of her dinner, and Vatu had been back for the plate. Since then she'd waited with nothing else to do. No book or Bible to read. She paced the floor and peered out the window until night had fallen. Then she lit the oil lamp, trimming the wick to a very low light.

As she turned, she bumped the top drawer of the dresser by accident, and it slid partway open. She certainly didn't want to be accused of touching Reva's things again, so her first instinct was to shut it. But then she saw the tiny piece of blue velvet again, peeking out of Reva's top drawer.

Was that what had made Reva so nervous the night before? And why? Now Abby was really curious. She couldn't help but peek—especially since the drawer was already open. What was a parlor maid doing with rich velvet clothing anyway?

Abby opened the drawer more and saw that the velvet was actually a small bag, with a cork peeking out of the top. She drew the cork out of the bag and discovered it was the stopper to a small glass vial. The liquid was clear. What could it be? *It must be perfume,* she thought. She unstoppered the bottle to smell it, but the liquid was odorless.

Then Abby heard a creak outside her room. She hurriedly opened the blue velvet bag and stuffed the bottle back in. Her hand hit something hard. Abby pulled the object out and gasped. It was a diamond-studded choker—the same one she'd seen in the pencil sketch so recently! The valuable necklace obviously belonged to royalty—not a parlor maid.

Abby thought back to the day she'd seen Reva coming out of the queen's quarters. Could Reva be a part of the plot against the queen that Jean-Paul said he'd overheard? Suddenly Abby thought of Tunui. He'd been in the queen's quarters, too, sneaking stealthily around the palace. . . . Was he in on the evil plan also?

Abby hoped not. Aimata trusted Tunui as a dear friend. And she was such a godly woman that Abby knew she'd be shocked by his betrayal, if he was in on the plot.

But what can I do about it? she asked herself. *I'm planning on leaving tonight. If I talk about this before I go, I might not be able to escape. And who would I tell anyway?*

Abby tiptoed to the window and parted the curtains again. Although it was dark outside, her eyes were used to the dim light and she could make out the guard beneath her window.

Where's Luke? He should have been here by now,
she worried. *What if something's happened to him?*

Abby paced the floor. *Ma and Pa are somewhere
off Mooréa by now, and I'm still trapped! And we've
got a long way to walk before dawn, when Chief Ono
will discover we're missing.*

She instinctively reached for her gold cross, as she
often did when deep in thought, and her hand
touched Luke's pearl. Abby's mind skittered in a
new direction. In a bad situation, act like an oyster,
she had told Jean-Paul. And what had Aimata said a
while ago? Something about finding things to be
grateful about.

She stopped pacing in the semidarkness and sat
on her bed near the door. "Oh, Lord," she whispered, "help Luke right now as he tries to figure out
what to do. Father, You're in control of everything.
So You must have a plan here—something that will
turn out for good, even though it feels so out of
control to me. Please help me trust You, and thank
You for my precious friend Luke."

She took a deep breath and realized she felt better.
Then she heard keys jangling just outside her door.
Abby lay down. Someone was speaking softly, almost
too softly to hear the words, but when Abby closed
her eyes she could make out bits and pieces.

A female voice was speaking in English. ". . . get
rid of her . . . then he give us . . . signal and we know
what—"

Abby strained to hear. The voice sounded like

Reva's. Then a man's harsh tone joined her. "It'll be poison or the knife. Wait for the signal . . . soon."

Abby's scalp prickled. The blood roared so loudly in her ears she could barely make out any more. *Who are they talking about? The queen or me?* And was that Tunui's voice? She couldn't be sure.

Abby's chest felt squeezed tight when she heard the key turn in the lock. Someone walked in, but Abby didn't dare open her eyes. She tried hard to breathe deeply and evenly. Footsteps walked toward the window. Reva spoke softly to the outside guard. "I here now; you can go. The family sail out for now, and she be asleep anyway."

How would Luke find her room if there was no guard to see? And even if he happened upon her room, how would Abby get by Reva?

Abby kept her eyes shut while Reva was at the washbasin. Abby heard her pulling out her dresser drawer and then changing into nightclothes. Finally she heard the woman get into bed and sigh. After 20 minutes her breathing became deep and regular. She was asleep.

Abby tucked two pillows under her covers, picked up her boots, and tied their laces together. She hung them around her neck and sneaked silently toward the window in her stocking feet. The breeze blew in softly. Reva still slept.

She parted the curtains and peeked out. No guard! She wanted to shout for joy. But instead she slowly climbed onto a nearby bed to make it easier to get one leg over the window ledge. The bed, with its crinkly straw tick, rustled. She stopped and listened, but Reva was snoring lightly. Abby hooked one leg awkwardly through the window, grabbed the window sash, and balanced on the ledge.

Bang! An explosion sounded in the distance. Abby jabbed her other leg through the window. Had the noise awakened Reva?

But no footsteps sounded. Abby heard a distant shout. It was time to get out or wait around for the parlor maid to wake up! She slid her head under the opened window, then jumped down three feet. She landed with a *thump,* quickly got up, and ran in stockings toward the nearest plumeria tree.

Hiding behind the tree, she untied her boots and laced them on her feet. Now she had to find Jean-Paul's window on the other side of the palace and see if Luke had distracted the guard.

Oh, please let Luke be there! What if Luke was the one who'd gotten distracted or caught? Hadn't he said there were spies everywhere?

Chapter Sixteen

The tree bark was rough against Abby's palms and the night air wonderfully cool after being cooped up indoors for so many hours. But in the distance, on the other side of the palace, she could hear men shouting. It was time to get moving! *Was that explosion Luke's distraction—or someone shooting at him?*

She began working her way around the grand mansion, scurrying from tree to tree. As she came near the back of the palace, she recognized the kitchen door. Someone was standing on the porch, his tall body outlined by lights from inside. Abby shrank back, her heart pounding.

Several men suddenly poured out of the kitchen doorway, their heavy footfalls filling her with dread. *Where's Luke?*

She had to get a view of Jean-Paul's room to see if the guard was still there—and maybe find Luke. But she'd better do it quickly. With all the palace guards swarming about, her chances of getting caught were escalating by the minute!

Abby thought she might be able to see Jean-

Paul's window from the stand of tall ferns up ahead.
She crouched and ran toward them, throwing
herself behind them as two guards came into view.
Trying to catch her breath, Abby leaned forward in
the dirt to spy out the situation when a firm hand
reached through one side of the huge fern and
clasped her wrist. Abby almost screamed, but Luke's
face burst through the greenery. His smile shone in
the moonlight.

Right behind him Jean-Paul grinned ecstatically.
"We are free, *mon amie!*" he whispered. "Now let's
go!"

Luke grabbed Abby's hand, and they all ran from
tree to shrub to palm. Within five minutes they'd
left the palace grounds and were heading north with
Jean-Paul leading the way. At this late hour, the
backstreets were quiet.

After 15 minutes, they pulled off the road and sat
behind a tree to catch their breath. "How'd you do
it?" Abby gasped out. "Distract them, I mean."

Luke and Jean-Paul began to giggle like school-
boys. "I hired a maid," Luke began, "who brought
her small herd of pigs onto the palace grounds right
by Jean-Paul's window. That's what took so long—
finding the right girl who had a herd of pigs to rent.
But when she untied them, we knew we'd found the
right girl!"

Abby rolled her eyes as the guys started laughing
harder. Luke was gasping for breath and trying to
continue. He wiped away a tear.

"She was an actress," he said. "She came up to the guard all flustered and weepy, then begged him to help her catch the oinkers, but—" here Luke had to catch his breath—"I'd greased all those pigs with a jug of coconut oil."

Abby began to giggle, which didn't help her catch her breath at all. "But, Luke, I heard a small explosion."

"I threw one of my firecrackers at several pigs, hoping to move them toward your side of the palace."

"What if the pigs didn't do what they were supposed to?" Abby asked. "How were you going to get me free?"

Jean-Paul leaned toward her. "He was going to risk getting caught himself, *mon amie*. Show her, Luke."

Luke held up a string of Chinese firecrackers. "They sell these at Papeete Market! Remember how they worked when we were in China?" His eyes positively sparkled with the plan. "I was going to set them off in the distance and have Jean-Paul help you out of your window. But it turned out we ran into you before that."

Abby clapped him affectionately on the back. "You're the best friend ever, you ol' swine-renting sailor."

Jean-Paul smiled. "Abby, it was a sight I will always remember—that guard being lured out by the pretty Tahitian maid who was chasing all those piglets."

Luke chuckled again. "You should've seen Jean-Paul come flying out that window as soon as the guard disappeared!"

"You do not have to invite me twice to leave that palace," the Frenchman said happily. "Now, let's be off. I put my pillow under the blankets, so perhaps they will think I am sleeping and not notice me missing until dawn."

"But dawn's not far off," Abby said, and they started up again. Twenty more minutes of hiking and her ankles were growing numb, but she pushed herself to keep walking. They were nearing the edge of Papeete now, and Jean-Paul directed them down a dirt road that led inland. "This ez it—the way to the captain's home," he said, pausing. Then he headed out ahead of them, motioning that they should follow. "*Oui,* I am sure of it."

Abby looked at Luke. "I hope he knows where we're going. I don't want to get captured again."

Luke shrugged and grabbed her arm. "Come on, lean on me," he said as they started up a little hill. Abby was grateful he always remembered she had a hard time with long hikes. Looking ahead at the incline, she knew she'd be glad to have him to lean on.

But the higher they climbed, the better the view. There were still a few lights on Boulevard Pomare, but much of the city now lay in darkness. The moon, sailing full and bright, reflected in the bay below.

"The captain's home, it ez above it all," Jean-Paul explained. "It will be a good place to catch the wind and sail out over the water." He pointed up ahead. "Not far now."

Twenty minutes later the ground leveled out, and they saw a one-story home in the distance. Although it was night, it had a deserted look.

"Doesn't he have a wife and family?" Abby asked.

"No. He keeps this place for the day he retires," Jean-Paul said. "My things are in that shed in the field there." Abby followed the direction of his gaze and made out a shed on the distant edge of a field. Surrounding this shelf of land were tall mountain peaks and, of course, the open road that led back to Papeete.

Jean-Paul and Luke immediately headed toward the distant shed, where Jean-Paul said there would be a crowbar to wrench open his huge wooden crates. But Abby had to sit and rest on the porch steps of the house. The wind was stronger up here, coming down from the mountains and sailing back out to sea.

Soon she pumped some water from the spigot in the front yard; then she joined the others. They had pried open the first wooden crate and had carted pieces of equipment into the field for assembling. Together they were balancing a giant wicker basket in their arms as Abby arrived. "What's that?" she asked.

"This ez the gondola in which we will ride," the Frenchman said. "It hangs under the balloon."

With Jean-Paul's injured hand it took a long time

to get everything out of the crate and into the field. Though the moon was bright, it was still dark enough to force them to go slowly.

Finally they all began assembling the giant lighter-than-air machine. Luke was transfixed with curiosity and interest.

"I just hope it flies and doesn't plunge us down a cliff." Abby swallowed anxiously.

Jean-Paul belly laughed, and Abby enjoyed the sound of it. "Oh, *mon amie*. You will love this flying—like a bird so free! There ez nothing like it."

Far off in the distance Abby heard a conch shell blow three times. She knew from her experiences in Hawaii that a conch always heralded something important. It could be a call to arms or, she thought grimly, a call to search for escaped prisoners.

Luke's eyes found Abby's. "I get the feeling we'd better hurry now."

"Me, too." Her gaze roved toward town. "Could we see someone coming, do you think? I can't see the road from here."

"It's pretty light out with this moon," Luke commented. "But we don't have a clear view of the road from here. If I ran past the house, I could check it out."

"That wouldn't give us much time to escape, though," Abby said.

Luke frowned. "Timing, as they say, is every-thing."

They began to work even more quickly. Obeying

Jean-Paul's instructions, they helped him connect the large wicker basket to the skeletal frame and lines. Metal pins were plunged into the dirt to tether the lighter-than-air machine to earth. Lines ran down the frame over the basket and through four metal rings attached to the gondola's tiny bottom ledge.

The rubberized-silk balloon was hauled in place by lines connected to a tall tree. Jean-Paul returned to the shed and the second crate. From it he dragged a long hose that he connected to the opening in the balloon. "This hydrogen gas will fill the balloon now," he said.

To Abby's delight the balloon began to take shape. In the first gray light of dawn, she smiled at Jean-Paul. "It looks like it's going to work after all!"

"Did you ever doubt me?" he said with a wink. "I must retrieve my supply of salt crackers and jerky and other things from the shed. You climb in, Abby, and arrange these blankets for us. Then you can find a place for the supplies I bring."

Abby, boosted by Luke into the gondola, began organizing the blankets Luke handed her. "Jean-Paul says it can get cold up high. But it's hard to imagine it being chilly anywhere in the South Pacific," he said.

From the city, noises and voices began to rise. Or were they coming from the road? Abby wondered. She heard dogs barking somewhere in the distance. "Do you hear that noise?"

"Hopefully they've just now discovered you're

missing, and those are just dogs chasing some chickens," Luke said.

Jean-Paul emerged from the shed, laden down with items. Luke ran to help. Jean-Paul reached the gondola and unhooked the hose. "The balloon ez full," he said. As soon as the hiss of the hydrogen filling the balloon ended, Jean-Paul cocked his head. "I hear dogs barking. I will take a look at the road, just to be sure."

"Okay," Luke said. "I'll stash these for you." He hurried back to Abby, handing her many more items, plus four more bottles of hydrogen. She quickly stacked them in a corner of the gondola on top of some coils of rope.

When Luke handed her four heavy sandbags, she asked, "What are these for?"

"Jean-Paul explained they're for ballast," Luke answered, "and when you jettison them, the balloon lifts higher."

In the morning breeze the balloon now lofted back and forth as the wind caught it. "Good thing she's tied down," Luke said, running his hands over a nearby tie line attached to a stake in the ground, "because this wind's picking up."

He no sooner finished the words when an unusually strong gust tugged hard at the giant balloon. It swayed crazily, and two lines went tight as the balloon leaned in the opposite direction. One stake tore free of the ground and shot through the air. Luke ducked just in time.

Abby's eyes careened toward the other stake on that side. It was inching out of the ground, too! "Oh no!" The second line wrenched free of the stake, and the rope spun wildly through the air. Luke leapt up to grab it but missed. The basket tilted sharply with the tie-downs gone on one side. With the strain on the two remaining stakes, Abby knew they'd quickly loosen.

"The wind's too strong!" Luke yelled at her. "Get out!"

Abby saw him dive for the third line just as it pulled free. He missed again!

She threw one leg over the side of the wicker basket, her stomach heavy with dread. *If this thing takes off, I'll be trapped in the air—alone!* Almost frozen with fear, she forced herself to pull up on the edge. But the balloon seemed to come alive—bouncing back and forth, up and down. The sudden bouncing knocked Abby backward. Her head popped back up as the fourth line tightened, then sagged.

It only took a second for her to realize the balloon was about to break free.

"Luke!" Abby threw a leg over the basket's edge again. She had no intention of flying alone. "Get me out of here!"

But the fourth line shot free of the earth, knocking Abby back down into the basket. She jumped up quickly, just in time to see Luke dive for the last line. He gripped it just as the balloon, no longer tied to earth, caught the uplift and began to rise.

I'm flying!

At that moment the sun crested the horizon, a golden ray slicing across the sea and Papeete City. Abby stared down at the ground receding beneath her.

Horrors!

The sunlight illuminated Luke's blond-streaked hair and his upturned face as he dangled from the line he'd captured.

Together they lifted up, up, and away.

Chapter Seventeen

Abby gasped. Luke was hanging by a thread!

"Oh, God, please help us!" she prayed out loud.

The look on Luke's upturned face terrified her. Was he slipping? Suddenly her attention was drawn to the ground under Luke. Jean-Paul was racing toward them, screaming in panic. And from 20 feet in the air, Abby could see why.

Baying dogs were tearing up the road leading to the house! Behind them men were barreling up the road with spears in their hands! They'd been discovered by Chief Ono's guards.

Jean-Paul's arms reached toward Luke, his voice desperate. "Come back! *Mon amie,* she is my balloon. My inheritance." He jumped and grabbed at the dangling lines, which were out of reach. "Don't leave me behind!"

Though the balloon was rising slowly, panic gripped Abby so firmly she couldn't think what to do. She leaned over and tried to pull Luke's rope up, but it was hopeless. She didn't have the strength to raise him. So she watched in terror as Luke wrapped a bottom portion of the line around his ankle with his foot, and then began climbing hand over hand up toward her.

Tears blurred Abby's view as she leaned over helplessly. Closer and closer Luke came. But it would only take one wrong move—his hands slipping on the line—for him to plunge to his death.

Meanwhile Jean-Paul leapt toward the dangling ropes that were 20, 30, now 40 feet beyond his reach. "Come back!"

Three dogs were in the lead. Though still on the road, they were approaching him at a fast clip. *In a few minutes, he'll be attacked. We need a miracle!*

Abby's thoughts were interrupted by Jean-Paul's voice. He was yelling something at her. What was it? "Turn the release valve!"

Abby's mind grappled with his words. *What valve?* She searched frantically, spotted a metal handle, yanked it quickly, and then let up. Instantly she heard a loud *whoosh* and the balloon began to sink.

Jean-Paul was running beneath the balloon, running straight toward the men and dogs! Abby could barely tear her gaze away from the coming cataclysm that was sure to erupt when he met the growling dogs and angry Tahitians.

The balloon suddenly dipped, and Luke screamed. *Oh no! He's fallen to his death!*

She threw herself half over the wicker edge to see. *Is Luke plunging to earth?*

Thank God, Luke was still there, hanging by his

fingers on to the small ledge at the bottom of the gondola! But he had no way to pull himself up any farther.

She had to rescue him, but how?

The coils of rope in the bottom of the gondola!

Abby moved the hydrogen bottles off the rope and tied an end around one of the gondola's metal spars. About eight feet down the line she tied a loop, then tossed the coil of rope over the side.

She leaned over the basket's edge. The balloon was 60 feet above ground, but they were descending quickly. At any moment they could hit an updraft rising off the land and Luke would be jarred loose!

"Luke," she yelled, "step into the loop and pull yourself up the rope." It would mean that Luke would have to trust that the loop would hold his weight and not slip. Could he even raise his leg, when all his concentration was focused on holding on to that two-inch rim?

Abby held her breath. Luke slowly raised his left foot. He couldn't find the loop! Abby kept moving it toward him, but it swung back. From below she could hear Jean-Paul screaming, but she couldn't look right now.

Luke's fingers were white. Fear raced through Abby. *I could lose him. Oh, please God, help him get his foot in the loop!* Three seconds later his foot connected. He stepped into the loop and rested his weight on the rope. Then he bravely let go of the ledge with one hand and lunged toward the rope.

He made it! With both hands gripping the line, he pulled himself up hand over hand. Seconds later he stepped onto the gondola's lip, then dived over the basket's edge and fell onto the floor.

Abby bent down next to him, trembling with relief. *He's alive!*

Luke reached out and hugged her for a second, then stood and tied a longer rope to dangle toward earth. "Jean-Paul needs all the chances he can get," he said, referring to the four lines that now dangled 25 feet below the gondola's bottom. Abby jumped up in time to see the dogs racing past the house now.

Jean-Paul was leaping and running beneath the balloon, which had lowered significantly. It was possible now for him to grab a line. But suddenly Abby remembered his injured hand! How could he possibly climb with that wound in his palm? A wave of nausea hit her as she watched the scene unfold, almost in slow motion.

By now the dogs had reached the edge of the meadow, and Jean-Paul was still running straight toward them. He leapt and missed one line, but the lines were low enough now. Indeed, if the balloon lowered any more, they'd be captured. A spear flew from one warrior's hand and came close to the gondola. If the balloon got lower and a spear found it, the fragile silk would rip. They could crash to their deaths.

But Abby could only think of Jean-Paul's desperate plight. "Jump!" she yelled.

He did, and this time his left hand closed around a line. Luke shouted encouragement, but Jean-Paul was still dangling within reach of the guards.

"The sandbags!" Abby shouted. She and Luke each picked up a heavy bag and threw them overboard, narrowly missing a guard. The balloon responded instantly by lifting 10 feet higher. The dogs reached Jean-Paul, but he was now sailing above them on a rope. The snarling canines leapt but missed.

The men with spears, however, were just seconds behind. Abby threw over another sandbag and the balloon shifted upward. Jean-Paul clung with two hands as the ground began to slope away beneath them. They passed screaming warriors. A spear left one man's burly arm and whizzed by Jean-Paul's ear. Abby closed her eyes.

When she opened them, she saw that Luke had tied a line about one spar of the gondola and also around his waist and was now going over the side. "No, Luke!" She couldn't face the prospect of his death again.

"I have to, Abby. He can't climb with that injury." Luke went over onto the ledge, lowering a loop just as Abby had done. Jean-Paul clung to his lifeline but stepped into the loop. Then he bravely switched his grip to the line Luke had lowered.

Luke was balanced on the gondola's lower lip but hanging forward into the air by a rope around his waist. Abby could barely stand to watch as again her friends' lives dangled 100 feet above the ground.

Gripping Jean-Paul's rope, Luke began hauling him up hand over hand. It took backbreaking effort, but it worked. Jean-Paul was pulled close enough to step onto the lip and grab the wicker basket. When he climbed in, and Luke behind him, Abby sat down on the blanket pile. She was trembling.

Luke bent down on a knee as Jean-Paul adjusted the few controls. "Abby, it's over now. We're all okay."

She nodded and looked into his gold-flecked green eyes. The compassion she saw there made tears well up, and her nose began to run. She wiped it with a blanket.

"It's okay," he murmured, patting her back. "You did great." Then he jumped up to see if Jean-Paul needed any help.

But Abby stayed quiet in the bottom of the gondola. "Thank You, God," she whispered. Gratitude for saving their lives welled up, along with fresh tears. Swallowing the lump of emotion that clogged her throat, she stood up to join them.

They were high above Papeete in the golden glow of dawn. Abby could see everything . . . the azure sea, beaches with white trimming along the coast, mountains, and the city.

"Flying like ze birds!" Jean-Paul shouted ecstatically. Down below—far, far away—they heard a conch shell blowing, but they had risen above the reach of the furious warriors.

"I don't know anyone who's flown before, do you, Abby?" Luke asked.

"No," she said, shaking her head. Her emotions were too raw to speak, but her thoughts flew faster than the balloon. *Here we are, safe in God's arms—safe in His will.*

Chapter Eighteen

They sailed hundreds of feet above the ocean for two hours, always heading west toward the peaks of Mooréa Island. The sky was clear, the sun warm.

They watched the white-capped ocean pass below, sometimes spying the large, dark shape of a whale at the surface. The retreating view of Tahiti was breathtaking, but after a while Abby turned toward Mooréa's island peaks. Even from a great distance she searched the distant coastline for the *Kamana*. She couldn't wait to see Ma, Pa, and even annoying little Sarah.

"I'll be ready for lunch when we get there," Luke said.

"What a surprise," she teased.

The island was coming up quickly now, and from this height, Abby could see a lovely aqua-blue lagoon. "There it is!" she shouted. A schooner rested on the water, close to a white-sand shore.

"Can you see anyone?" Luke asked. "Are you sure it's the *Kamana*?"

"Not yet, but soon you will know," Jean-Paul assured them as he busied himself with the handles. The balloon began to fall, and Abby realized it was none too soon if they hoped to land on the beach and not into the side of a mountain.

"We're coming in too quickly," Luke said, his eyes widening with concern.

"*Oui*, this ez not an exact science," Jean-Paul admitted. "That ez why we call it an adventure. And also why it's described as a 'crash landing.'"

"Crash landing?" Abby questioned.

"*Oui*, but the basket absorbs much of the impact." Jean-Paul released more hydrogen, they lowered farther, and Abby shifted her gaze to the beach.

"There's the family!" she said. Sarah was jumping up and down on the sand, and everyone else was waving wildly.

The balloon now skimmed over the coral break-water where the deep blue met the pale turquoise water. A fringe of white lacy waves broke on a coral reef, but there were gaps where the anchored ship had sailed through.

They flew so low over the lagoon's crystal sea that they could see coral heads dotting the bottom. "Look," Luke shouted. "I can see some big fish!"

Abby simply gripped the basket edges and kept her eyes glued to the shore. "It's Ma and Pa!"

They swooped in closer, closer, closer. For a

moment Abby dared to hope that all would go well. She drank in the dear familiar faces and the incredible beauty of Moaréa, which, if possible, was even more lovely than Tahiti.

But then to Abby's horror she realized they'd never make the beach!

"We're going to hit the water!" was the last thing she heard Luke say. Then the bottom of the gondola crashed into the water, sucking the rest of it downward. The balloon barreled on momentarily, tipping over the basket. Abby fell forward onto the basket's side. Something heavy came down on her, and cool seawater gushed around her.

The balloon overhead continued to pull the gondola toward shore, but the basket kept them trapped as it plowed sluggishly through the lagoon.

"Luke!" Abby's opened mouth earned her a throatful of stinging salt water. She gasped and clawed to get air, but the basket contents had her trapped. Water covered her head.

Abby kicked to get free, to get air. But the gondola was propelled forward like a sieve being sucked through water. Someone behind her had a hold of her and was trying to move her forward, but Abby was choking on salt water, coughing and drinking in more. Her lungs burned for relief, for air. If she didn't get it she knew she'd die.

Then the world turned black and silent.

Luke saw what was coming and took a big breath of air as the gondola hit the sea and turned sideways. He'd grabbed the back of Abby's dress as she flew face first onto the side of the gondola. He was crushed against her as the water filled the basket and dragged them forward. The balloon overhead would keep flying and pulling them through the water, he figured, unless it hit the sea and became waterlogged.

He tried to push Abby up to escape the confines of the basket. But now he knew the force of water rushing into the basket was too great. He held on to her dress so he wouldn't lose her and prayed to stay conscious. But he knew his air was running out. His lungs burned for air!

Just as he thought he could stand no more, the basket slowed and tipped downward a bit more. Grabbing Abby by the back of the dress, Luke pulled her firmly out the opening, swimming down momentarily to escape.

Air! It was his only thought, his driving need! The sea surged, and he kicked upward, dragging Abby with him.

But she'd passed out and was deadweight.

You can't drown, Abby!

Struggling toward the surface, Luke popped up, only to be met by a smothering fabric. The balloon!

He got a ragged breath of air beneath the canopy and dived down again, swimming toward the light just a few feet away. When he popped up this time, he choked, then gasped air painfully. Abby lay deathly still in his arms, her eyes closed, hair floating like brown seaweed about her, waves sloshing over her face.

Suddenly Duncan surfaced near the edge of the waterlogged balloon and lit into strong strokes. He drew Abby's lifeless body to him and began stroking one-handed to shore. Abby's pa suddenly arrived to help as Luke followed behind him. Soon Duncan was in knee-deep water. Mr. Kendall took Abby from him and struggled to the sand, where Abby's ma and Sarah threw themselves down next to Abby and turned her on her side.

Sarah began sobbing.

Luke stood over them, rigid with fear. Abby was so pale, so still. *God, she's dying!*

Mrs. Kendall hit Abby on the back over and over, then pushed in on her stomach. Water spilled from Abby's mouth, and a cough broke out of her. Two coughs. She turned her head and coughed up water. As Abby took her first gasping breath in over a minute, Abby's ma raised her to a sitting position, then crushed her in an embrace.

Luke's knees buckled with relief and he fell to the sand.

The first thing Abby saw when she opened her eyes was Duncan, dripping wet, his black eye patch askew on his forehead. She'd never seen the neatly dressed Scotsman look so stricken or disheveled. *Why is Duncan so wet?* she wondered. His one good eye held steady on her, and the lips under his handlebar moustache were moving in what Abby knew must be prayer. When she smiled at him, his face crumpled with emotion.

Abby glanced to the left and saw Luke kneeling behind Ma. His face was white with fear, and tears escaped the corners of his eyes. Then suddenly the whole family was there, hugging her. Sarah was screaming with joy and pounding her painfully on the back. "I'll help you get that water out, Abby!" *Whack!* "Wow, you should've seen the crash!"

Pa unwrapped Ma's arms and took a turn hugging Abby to himself. "Princess," he said, gazing tenderly at her. Uncle Samuel and Lani stood in line, waiting their turn, and Abby couldn't tell if they were laughing or crying. Sandy barked and jumped with excitement, perhaps to warn everyone that a monster bird had just fallen from the sky.

Passed from arms to arms, Abby saw Duncan taking in the scene. She loved him as much as anyone else in the family. *He is family,* she thought possessively, *and we're lucky to have him.*

"Good thing Duncan jumped in, Abby," Luke said. "He got you to shore."

Abby stood up and walked through the sand toward Duncan. She didn't say a word as he turned toward her, just wrapped her arms around him in a soggy hug. They stood like that for a minute until Duncan patted her back awkwardly, his voice husky with emotion. "Thank God, lassie. Thank God."

Jean-Paul had escaped unharmed by leaping at the last moment into the water. Pa, Duncan, and Uncle Samuel were as wet as Abby and Luke, since they had swum out to her. But even Ma, Lani, and Sarah were wet up to their waists, so as soon as the men had pulled the gondola out of the water using her lines and had secured her to some sturdy trees, they rowed out to the *Kamana* to get dry clothes for everyone.

Within an hour, a picnic blanket had been laid out in the shade of some palms and the family bowed in prayer. Pa asked Duncan to pray over the meal, but he choked up with gladness and had to shorten his thanks to God.

When Abby looked up, she was amazed to see that even Jean-Paul had bowed his head. Then the picnic began. All the preparation for Lani and Samuel's wedding had at least resulted in the *Kamana* being provisioned with delicious food. After a hearty meal, Ma made Abby and Luke go back to the ship and their own berths for a long nap.

Sarah grinned at that bit of news. "Ha! I don't have to take a nap," she informed her sister.

Abby gazed at her with tired red eyes. "And I can't wait to take one."

Sarah looked crestfallen for a second, then brightened. "But you don't know what the surprise is when you wake up," she taunted.

"Give me a hint?" Abby said, playing along.

Sarah crossed her arms over her chest. "Nope. You'll have to wait and see."

Abby hoped it was not a stern lecture from Pa on taking matters into her own hands, which of course, she'd done by going to the palace with Luke. Things had been so hectic, Abby thought wearily. Maybe her parents would forget about that.

But as Sarah walked her down to the bunk they shared and tucked her in with a sheet, Abby didn't care what the surprise would be. She was just happy to be back in her own bunk.

It seemed Abby had just closed her eyes when a loud voice carried through her open porthole. "Ahoy, *Kamana*! Show yourselves. We need to speak to your captain. The ruler of Tahiti requires your presence."

Abby sat up and noted that Sarah had returned. Her slate-blue eyes rounded with wonder at the voice booming in. They both popped up to peer out the tiny porthole at once, crashing their heads together. "Ow!" Sarah complained, but she pulled back and Abby caught a glimpse of a grand schooner entering the lagoon.

Sailors in uniform flooded the deck and climbed the shrouds, taking in sail and tossing out the small anchor to bring it to a halt. A man in a dark blue uniform with a gold braid held a horn to his lips. "You are commanded to return to Papeete."

Spotting Vatu on deck, Abby's heart sank. She leapt from her bunk.

She and Luke reached the hatch stairs at nearly the same time and hurried topside. "Trouble," he muttered.

Everyone was on board, even Jean-Paul. There was no sense in hiding while his balloon was in plain sight. Then Abby saw Lani standing near Uncle Samuel. She was dressed in her gorgeous silk wedding gown. So that was what the surprise was to be, Abby realized. Right after her nap, they were to have a wedding. But now it had been postponed again. *Oh, poor Lani!*

Pa raked a hand through his dark blond hair and Ma hung close to his side. "What do they want, Thomas?" she asked.

"Apparently, they've come after us," he said, "and are demanding we return with them to Papeete."

"Do we have to go?" Ma asked, even as Duncan hailed them from the bow.

Pa pointed to the eight cannons on the schooner's side and the armed guards standing at attention on board. "It looks that way, Charlotte."

Ma put a protective arm around Sarah.

Luke's eyes darkened. "This can't be good."

Abby gazed silently back at the royal yacht. They had made it—escaped crazy Chief Ono only to be caught again. Only an hour or so earlier she'd been so thankful to be alive and to have her family safely gathered around her. But what was in store for them now? she wondered.

Then she caught sight of Tunui standing on deck, his massive arms crossed over his bare chest.

And Abby knew things had definitely taken a turn for the worse.

Chapter Nineteen

Before they sailed out of Mooréa's enchanted lagoon they had dragged the gondola on board the rowboat, which was now trailing their schooner. The semi-full balloon had dried and risen upward, but the men had tied it securely in and weighted the rowboat down with stones and coconuts so it wouldn't lift off.

In spite of the seriousness of the situation and Lani's sad face, Abby couldn't help but be amused at the sight of the balloon riding the rowboat behind the *Kamana*.

It took several hours to sail back to Papeete Harbor. During that time, Duncan had come to explain to the whole crew that the government representative had commanded them to wear their finest clothes for a meeting with someone important. "Who?" Pa wanted to know.

"He wouldn't say, but it could be Chief Ono."

"Maybe it's the queen," Abby said hopefully. She remembered that Rahiti thought highly of her. Perhaps she had returned and would help them.

The sun was beginning its descent as they sailed into Papeete Harbor to the unnerving sound of conch shells blowing. The royal schooner docked first and the *Kamana* docked behind it.

Tunui and six other men, all dressed in uniforms of black and red and carrying swords, came toward them as Duncan let down the gangplank. "We will escort you," Tunui said seriously. Abby swallowed hard as she noted his weapon. *Which side is he on?* she wondered. *Is he part of the terrible scheme I overheard Reva discussing? And if so, what will Chief Ono do to us?*

Abby, Sarah, and Ma had donned their expensive silk dresses from China. Lani, apparently thinking she might never get another chance to wear it, had left on her lovely white gown. Their skirts rustled as they walked solemnly through the harbor area, where people stepped out of their way. The procession came to a halt at Boulevard Pomare, where carriages waited. "Please get in," Tunui ordered. Duncan, Ma, Pa, and Sarah were ushered into one carriage, with Abby, Luke, Lani, Uncle Samuel, and Jean-Paul into the other. The carriage started up with a jerk, and the familiar sound of horses' hooves lulled Abby for a few minutes.

She wished she could think of something wise and encouraging to say to Lani. But she could think of nothing to cheer her, so she just reached across the aisle and grabbed Lani's hands in an encouraging squeeze. Lani smiled back at her.

Jean-Paul leaned next to Abby and whispered, "I see that you were right. Your uncle is a very lucky man indeed."

Abby glanced up at him. "How are you doing, Jean-Paul?" *This must be pure torture to the Frenchman,* she thought. Freedom had been within reach.

He sighed and stroked his dark moustache. "I am trying to become an oyster. A very large oyster that can accommodate a gigantically irritating grain of sand."

Abby grinned in spite of herself and reached for her pearl. "Thank you," she whispered, "for reminding me." Then she closed her eyes. *What an incredible mess,* she thought. *But I know God wants us to be grateful in every circumstance. If only I can find something to be thankful for.*

Abby raised her head and glanced out the carriage window. They were close to the palace. She could see the edge of the palace grounds now in the diminishing light. As the carriage drew to a stop, the driver jumped down and opened the door. Jean-Paul stepped out first, followed by Luke. Uncle Samuel went next, turning back to help his lovely bride down the step in her gown. Abby followed to carry Lani's train.

As soon as she alighted, Abby turned toward the palace grounds, and her mind careened to a stop. The last golden rays fell diagonally across the green grass, but a red carpet had been rolled out before the carriage. Situated ahead of them on the wide lawn were two large fluttering pavilions and 100 *tiki* torches already burning brightly. There were banners flying from the pavilions—the lovely red-and-white flag of Tahiti. What could it mean?

Tunui held out an arm to Abby and began to escort her down the red carpet. Abby felt like a princess as she stepped on the plush carpet. Luke, dressed in his finest pants and a Chinese silk shirt, and Jean-Paul followed. But when Abby turned to sneak a look at Luke, he was ruining the elegance of the moment, for his mouth hung open like a barn door.

Before they reached the pavilion, several lovely Tahitian girls stepped forward and draped fragrant leis around their necks. Everyone also was crowned with *tiaré* wreaths upon their heads. *What's going on?* Abby wondered. *Is this the required clothing for meeting an important chief, or perhaps royalty?*

But she didn't have to wonder longer for they were brought under the open-sided pavilion. Two hundred Tahitians sat in chairs and pews inside the tent, which fluttered in the breeze. Sitting near the front of the pavilion was a thronelike chair. It was empty.

Tunui stopped Abby and her family at the front row, then walked forward and stood at attention near the empty throne. He rapped an intricately carved pole three times on the wooden dais upon which the throne sat. "All rise in honor of Queen Pomare!"

As one, the people stood up. Trumpeting conch shells blew. From the side entrance a dark-haired woman entered, her pale blue silk skirts rustling around her. Abby, who was whispering to Luke, didn't catch her face right away. Not until she turned and seated herself did Abby gasp out loud.

The queen of Tahiti, elegantly dressed and crowned with diamonds, was none other than Aimata!

Abby stared hard at the lovely woman who sat smiling at her. Pieces began to fall into place. The portrait she and Jean-Paul had almost finished . . . it was Aimata at a very young age! But why had she kept her identity hidden? And why had she left the palace to stay with Mahoi's family?

Queen Pomare pointed with her scepter to the empty chairs in the front row of the large pavilion. "Abby, you and your family are my honored guests. Please be seated here, near me."

Luke grabbed Abby's hand and pulled her to the pew. Everyone followed and Aimata nodded in approval. "I have called this gathering for two purposes," she said. "First, I wish to honor my new friends who helped me in my hour of need." Here she gazed at Abby, Luke, and Sarah, who Abby just now realized had saved the life of a queen!

"And second, it is time for a joyous and long-awaited wedding." When Aimata turned her serene smile on Lani and Uncle Samuel, Abby heard Lani gasp.

"My own dear pastor is here to perform the ceremony, with your permission," Aimata continued.

Uncle Samuel, dressed in a silk shirt, the very gift Aimata had sent him, bowed at the waist. "Thank you, Your Majesty."

Now attendants came and escorted Lani and Duncan from the pavilion for a brief time while musicians carrying guitars, gourd drums, and flutes took their place at the front, below the queen. A dignified-looking man, whom Abby figured must be the pastor, came to stand near Aimata. He held an open Bible in his hands. As Uncle Samuel was directed to join him, lovely Tahitian music began playing.

Duncan, who looked distinguished and proud, escorted his half sister, Lani, down the center aisle. Abby and Sarah grabbed each other's hands and watched the lovely bride. Lani carried a white orchid and *tiaré* bouquet, which had been prepared for her. She was a vision, crowned in white *tiaré* blossoms with her long mahogany hair swaying past her waist. Her turquoise eyes shone with a new joy and excitement.

Abby could see that all of Lani's dreams were coming true. She grinned at Ma, who clutched Pa's handkerchief and dabbed her moist eyes.

When Duncan reached the pastor, he handed Lani over to Uncle Samuel. Prayers were said, a hymn was skillfully played, and then vows were given.

"I, Samuel Kendall, promise to love, cherish, and protect you, Lani Kamana, all the days of my life because *Ua here vau ia oe*—I love you."

Abby could see tears threatening to spill from Lani's shining eyes.

"I, Lani Kamana, promise to love, honor, and

cherish you, Samuel Kendall, all the days of my life," she whispered, "because I love you, too."

And when the queen rose from her throne with a Tahitian quilt and wrapped it around the newlyweds, the pastor pronounced that "the two had become one." Then Abby and Sarah had to borrow hankies from Luke and Duncan.

Soon the bride and groom were escorted to the next pavilion, where dining tables were set up. Abby learned that she, her family, and Jean-Paul were the honored guests at the queen's own table. Alongside them sat Rahiti, Ruth, Mahoi, and Orama, which thrilled Sarah no end. Uncle Samuel gazed adoringly at his beautiful new wife, who couldn't seem to take her eyes off him either.

So tired was Abby from lack of sleep, however, that she completely forgot all of her concerns and gave herself up to the happiness of the moment. Seated closest to Queen Pomare, Abby leaned back, quietly watching Aimata talking kindly to Lani, who sat on her other side. *She always struck me as a great woman,* Abby mused, *and I suppose this time my hunch was right.*

Finally Aimata turned her gracious smile on Abby and whispered, "When I was informed of your ordeal at my own palace, I returned immediately to my throne and sent Tunui to get you. I'm so sorry for the terrible things Chief Ono did."

Abby's gaze shifted beyond Queen Aimata. Tunui was standing at attention behind her, but beyond him in the shadows stood Chief Ono. He had his ever-present whip in one hand. It beat nervously against his left palm. "Jean-Paul suffered far more than me, Queen Aimata. But you have let Chief Ono go free?"

The queen gripped Abby's hand and spoke softly. "He will not go free after tonight. But I am hoping and praying he shows his hand. I must catch those who are rebelling with him. If I arrest him now, I will only have one rebel caught."

"How could they want to overthrow you?" Abby asked. Here was a queen worth serving!

"I believe Chief Ono wants my throne not only to rule but also to fight the French. But that is hopeless. There are many of them and few of us left. I will not willingly send any more Tahitians to their death. I feel strongly about protecting the precious few who remain. And though we don't have everything, we do have the most important thing. Our God. In Him there is freedom—and a peace the world cannot give."

Jean-Paul, sitting on the other side of Abby, nodded at the queen. "Well said, Your Majesty. May your God grant all your heart's desires." He paused, for at that moment Chief Ono walked toward the banquet table carrying two items.

When the chief nodded, a conch shell was blown and all eyes looked up as he approached the queen. He held up the portraits of the queen's parents and announced, "These are my gifts to you, my queen." He bowed, but when he raised his head, Abby thought his hooded eyes were as cold as a shark's. Looking around as if enjoying the attention, Chief Ono backed away.

"What do you think of the painting of your father, King Pomare II?" Jean-Paul asked.

Aimata inclined her head. "I shall treasure it. You captured a look in his eye that brings a smile to my face. He was a good man, my father. It's very unusual—don't you think—for a king to translate the Bible? He was not only the first to believe in our land, but he translated God's Word into our own Tahitian language when I was a child. I am very proud of him for that."

Abby shook her head in amazement. "What a gift he gave to his people."

"And that is why," the queen said, "even though my people endure hardship, I will obey God's Word. I have seen God do marvelous things in my lifetime."

Abby caught the reflective look on Jean-Paul's face. It seemed the queen's words had gone deep into his soul.

"Jean-Paul," the queen continued quietly, "surely you know you are free to go. Please accept my apologies for the wrongs done to you while I was away. I had to leave, you see. Tunui had heard rumors of a spy in the palace and a plot to overthrow me. Even though we knew Chief Ono was overstepping his power, I stayed away, hoping he would reveal his hand while I was gone. We hoped that his spies would show their hand while I was gone."

Jean-Paul showed keen interest as he leaned toward her. "And did they, Your Majesty? Did you uncover the plot?"

"Alas, we did not. We only discovered the evil done to you and Abby, which is why I returned. The chief makes a great show of his 'loyalty' to me, as he did just now, but it's clear he has abused his power as my cousin. He's always wanted the throne, and I suspect that if he had it, he'd start another war with the French."

Abby's blood thundered in her temples. Was this the time to tell everything she knew—here at Lani's wedding dinner? Perhaps it could wait until after the meal, when she could speak in private to Queen Aimata and tell her that she had seen something suspicious in Reva's possession. One other thought plagued her: Could Tunui be part of the rebel plot?

But the queen and Jean-Paul were laughing about something Abby had missed. In the happy atmosphere, with servants constantly plying the next course to each one at the head table, Abby sat back and relaxed. She noticed that Tunui stood behind the queen, his legs spread apart, his dark, handsome eyes roving to and fro, watching protectively. Abby decided she would ask for a private audience with the queen after the feast.

Waiters cleared Abby's plate and brought a new course. A fresh plate was placed before her with shark and oysters arranged in a creative display.

"Ah," Queen Aimata said to Abby, "shark is my

favorite." She turned, evidently to see why her plate had not yet arrived.

Abby knew it was customary for the queen's plate to be brought before any other's. So she turned to look, too.

Then a hand laid a lovely platter before the queen, who picked up her silver fork.

But Abby glanced at the server—and gasped. It was none other than Reva! Abby's thoughts began to race. Reva had not served all evening. So why would the parlor maid suddenly be serving this one plate for the queen? Abby searched behind Reva and saw Chief Ono standing and watching with an unusual intensity. Her mind struggled to figure it out, but she had missed so much sleep that her mind felt sluggish.

Then as a lightning bolt suddenly reveals the darkened landscape, awareness hit. Abby leapt up from her chair so violently it fell backward. She struck the fork from the queen's hand. The food, which had almost entered the queen's mouth, went flying toward Tunui. Queen Aimata stared dumbstruck at her, but Abby shouted and pointed at Reva's disappearing back.

"She's the one!" Abby screamed. "The one who stole your diamonds and is trying to poison you!"

Chapter Twenty

Queen Aimata rose, and Tunui instantly was beside her, his sword unsheathed and glittering. Abby gasped in fear. Was he going to use it to defend or hurt the queen? But he jumped in front of her with the sword upraised in defense.

Luke and Rahiti leapt up and ran past the queen, racing out of the pavilion after the fleeing Reva. Other loyal men followed them.

Abby stood aghast at all that had occurred. When she saw Chief Ono drop his whip and step backward into the darkness, she pointed. "Don't let him escape!"

Jean-Paul flew from his chair, his face fiercely determined. He lunged at Chief Ono, knocking him forward and tumbling to the ground with him. Abby followed to see Chief Ono kick hard, loosening the artist's grip. As he crawled away, Abby lunged toward the bullwhip. Even as Chief Ono began to run, Abby called out, "Jean-Paul, the whip!" She tossed it to him, and in one fluid turn, he caught it by the handle and raised it high. A shriek sounded as he lashed its leather tongue through the air. It struck Chief Ono's lower leg, wrapping around it like an octopus arm.

Jean-Paul flicked the line back, and the chief's leg was pulled out from under him. He sprawled forward onto the grass, where Duncan collected him none too gently. "Wharf rrrat!" the Scotsman muttered as he pushed the Tahitian back toward the queen's pavilion.

Abby glanced back at the queen and finally breathed a sigh of relief. Tunui stood guard like an avenging angel. He was just as he had originally seemed. A man so loyal to Aimata that he would lay down his life for her. Just as he had almost done when he'd saved her from the shark.

Abby moved over to sit by Lani, Uncle Samuel, and her parents. "Has this ruined your wedding?" Abby asked softly.

"Ruined it?" Lani said with a joyous smile. "Nothing can ruin this wonderful moment. We *finally* are married."

"Queen Pomare has arranged a private honeymoon for us," Uncle Samuel added, uncharacteristically brief. "So we'll see you in three days." He took Lani's hand and they walked away together, hand in hand.

No sooner had they left than Luke, Duncan, and many other men pushed the three prisoners into the pavilion's light. Chief Ono, Reva, and her brother, Teva, stood before the queen.

"We are innocent and have done nothing wrong!" Reva shouted angrily.

"You may prove your innocence," the queen offered, "by eating my meal." Her eyes glittered with the challenge.

Reva swallowed convulsively. She took a step backward but was grabbed by a guard.

Teva raised shifty eyes around the pavilion. "I be not a part of their scheme!" he insisted. "It all Chief Ono's plan and hers."

"So the truth comes out," Queen Aimata said.

"Traitor!" Reva shouted. "If you think Teva is innocent, check the trunk in his room. You will find a list of the other rebels and your missing jewelry."

"All except the diamond choker," Abby corrected, "which is in Reva's top drawer."

"So that's what you were doing in the queen's quarters," Tunui said to Reva with a grimace. "I suspected it when I came to gather her things."

Ma turned surprised eyes on Abby while the three traitors were removed from the queen's presence. "Darling, I'm so proud of you."

Duncan, who'd come to sit back down, grinned at her, too. "Ye'd make a bonnie prrrivate investigator," he said with a wink.

It had been three days since Lani and Uncle Samuel had been married and the rebel plot revealed. They

finally understood that Chief Ono had given the gifts
of the portraits to look loyal in front of the people,
just before he would poison the queen. Then he
would have their support as he led them into a
doomed war. Queen Pomare, however, was now safe
and she had pledged all her help to Abby's family and
Jean-Paul, who had discovered the traitors for her.

With all the royal help at his disposal, Jean-Paul
had made improvements on his balloon and had
been given supplies of every type. Now he was free
to fly the South Pacific skies and map the wondrous
islands he so longed to visit and record.

Queen Aimata had planned a lavish send-off, so
she'd had his balloon moved to the palace grounds.
The grand lawns had been covered with chairs. Abby
sat with her parents, Sarah, and Duncan on her left,
and Luke on her right. She gazed at the balloon waft-
ing gently in the early morning trade winds and
thought of all she had learned while in Tahiti. She
would miss her French painter. He had taught her
how to paint portraits, a rare gift indeed. He'd given
her most of his paints, keeping only what he needed
for his mapmaking. The queen had packed them up
for Abby and had them delivered to the *Kamana* at
the dock.

Abby sighed and leaned toward Luke. "This has
been a heavenly vacation," she said.

Luke rolled his eyes. "Yep, all except for your
imprisonment, crash-landing into the sea, you
almost drowning, and the lecture we both got

yesterday from your parents." He stroked his chin in thought. "I guess we did survive it all, but I can't wait to set sail today. Duncan says with November fast approaching, the weather will soon be taking a foul turn. It's their stormy season now."

Abby pretended to be bored. "Did you say November's almost here?"

"Yes," Luke said, obviously annoyed. "Some people forgot that October was an important month."

"Whatever for?" Abby asked, though she had to smother the smile that was tugging at her.

"Oh, nothing . . ." Luke kicked grass blades with his boot toe and glanced away.

Abby winked at Sarah, who was waiting for a signal from Tunui. The queen's bodyguard nodded, and Sarah lifted the lid of a huge wicker basket. Out flew 20 white doves. They circled above the elated crowd in a dance of feathered beauty.

Sarah squealed with delight, the crowd *oohed,* and even Tunui broke into a wide grin.

"Wow," Luke breathed as his eyes followed the white wings rising against the blue.

The royal band struck up a rousing tune and Queen Aimata, dressed in a royal silk gown, arrived to the cheers of her many subjects.

As she walked toward them, Luke leaned into Abby's ear. "I think you're one of her best friends now," he whispered. "She's always making a fuss over you."

Queen Aimata didn't stop in front of Abby,

however, but before Luke. Abby tried not to smile as Luke's eyes widened with surprise. "Your Majesty," he said, bowing his head in respect.

The queen smiled. "Happy birthday, Luke Quiggley, friend of Tahiti. May you live long upon this earth and remember you are loved by the Tahitian people, who have heard of your loyalty to me."

Abby watched his face. He was smitten. The queen then handed him an intricately carved paddle. A royal red tropic bird feather hung from it. "Remember us here in the South Seas, and return to us whenever you can."

"Thank you." Luke looked like he wanted to hug her, so Queen Aimata hugged him first. The crowd cheered and Abby knew it was the best birthday party her orphaned friend had ever had. She pulled out from under her chair another gift for him. A gift she'd worked hard on over the past three days, with Jean-Paul's help.

"What's this?" Luke asked.

"Open it and see," she urged him. Luke untied the string and opened the banana-leaf wrapping paper.

He was so quiet that at first Abby feared he didn't like it. "Did you paint this?" he asked, staring at the blue-green underwater image. Coral, fish, oysters, and even a moray eel were captured forever on the canvas.

"It's that place where you found my pearl." Inwardly Abby cringed as she remembered how she'd acted when she thought Luke had lost the lovely gem. Especially when Luke had so often risked his life for her. *God, help me never to be mean to him again!*

"I love it, Abby."

"Now," Sarah piped up, "time for the cake!"

Two hours had passed and all 200 people had eaten their fill of cake and guava-nectar punch. Lani and Uncle Samuel had arrived back from their honeymoon in time for Jean-Paul's send-off. Now that it was time for him to go, sadness swelled in Abby's heart. She didn't know how to say what she felt.

"Well," Jean-Paul began, "everything is packed."

"Are you happy to be off?" Abby asked, with her family standing around.

"*Oui,*" he said, smoothing his dark moustache. "Happy but sad, too. Remember how I said the only thing more important than love to a Frenchman ez his freedom?"

"*Oui,*" Abby said, grinning.

"Perhaps I was hasty to say that. Perhaps I have learned that love might even be more important than freedom."

Duncan shook Jean-Paul's hand gently. "In my book, I've discovered that love *is* the greatest freedom," he said wisely.

Jean-Paul's eyes lit up. "I think you are right, Duncan." He turned to the others. "Good-bye, dear friends. Perhaps we shall meet again on some other island." He clapped Luke on the shoulder, then kissed Abby's hand.

Jean-Paul walked to his lighter-than-air machine and climbed in. Tahitian men kneeled and began untying the lines that bound his flying contraption to the earth. Suddenly Jean-Paul looked at Abby and motioned for her to come quickly.

She ran to the gondola and grabbed its edge as it began to dance and move. Jean-Paul leaned close to her ear, so only she could hear. "You remind me of my dear grandpapa with your talk of the Bible, Abby. I will remember your words. I will remember to be an oyster. Through prayer I will turn those things that aren't so good into a beautiful pearl, *oui?*"

Abby bit her lip and tried not to cry. She nodded and whispered, "You are a dear friend, Jean-Paul." As the gondola began to rise, Abby stepped back and blew a farewell kiss. "Good-bye!"

From above the treetops she heard the happy Frenchman shout, "*Au revoir*—good-bye!"

The balloon caught the updrafts and spun quickly out over the water. Indeed, it seemed that he flew by God's leave, straight toward heaven.

Chapter Twenty-One

Queen Aimata had done an amazing thing. She had accompanied Abby, Luke, and Sarah in her own carriage to the dock. The Kendall parents were already on board readying the ship for sail.

In the privacy of her carriage, Luke and Sarah had said their good-byes. Sarah had chirped happily and made the queen laugh. Luke had thanked her again for the paddle and kissed her cheek.

Now only Abby remained with Queen Aimata in her carriage.

As Luke and Sarah waved from the dock, Abby reflected on all Aimata had taught her. Surely God had used their trip here for good, even though there were moments Abby had wondered how He could.

When Aimata smiled at her, Abby's heart flooded with warmth. "Queen Aimata," she said, "Jean-Paul and I finished this for you." Abby lifted a large cloth-wrapped package from beneath the carriage seat and handed it to Aimata.

As the queen pulled away the cloth, her eyes lit with joy. "It's a painting of me at my coronation!"

"You were very young when you took the throne," Abby said, delighted that the queen was pleased with the painting she so recently had finished.

Queen Aimata's face softened. "I was 14—your age exactly, Abby Kendall. My dear father had died, and I wasn't at all sure I could take his place. But God has been with me, just as He has always helped you, too."

The queen took a small ironwood box from the seat beside her and placed it in Abby's hands. "Please remember me by this, as I will think of you every time I enjoy your painting."

Abby lifted the lid and gasped. Inside the foot-square box mother-of-pearl bracelets, hair combs, and buttons shone like pale rainbows. There were black pearl earrings set in silver and a necklace of delicate tiny black pearls. She shook her head in wonder.

The queen reached out a hand and laid it on Abby's. "You must take it. Share it with your mother, Sarah, and Lani, if you want."

Abby swallowed hard, her eyes glistening with unshed tears. "Even without this reminder, I could *never* forget you. I want to be like you—someone who always hopes in God no matter what." Abby leaned toward the queen and hugged her. Feelings of admiration for her noble friend swelled in her throat like a cotton ball, but she managed to whisper, "Thank you," as she stepped out of the carriage.

Then she hurried up the wharf toward her waiting ship.

"There's something nice about heading home," Duncan said to Abby two hours later. She and Luke were keeping the Scotsman company at the helm as they sailed north toward Hawaii, where they would trade at one of the world's busiest ports. The freedom of sailing, with the wind whipping through her curls, felt wonderful.

"I agree it's nice," Abby said as she patted the puppy's silky head.

"Hey," Luke said, glancing at her hand, "you're wearing your white pearl ring. And it's not a special occasion."

"I'm not saving it for 'special days' anymore." She leaned over to pull Sandy up on the bench next to her. Taking the pup's face in her hands, she explained, "Every day is a special occasion when we remember to act like oysters, right, girl?"

Duncan removed one hand from the wheel and rubbed his jaw. "What on earth are ye talking about, lassie?"

Luke grinned. "She means if we keep our eyes on God during a bad circumstance, He'll help us turn problems into pearls, right, Abby?"

Duncan's lips twitched into a smile beneath his dark moustache. "If ye've learned that, then it's been a more productive trrrip to Tahiti than I real-ized."

"But chances are," Abby said, "life will get boring when we get back to civilization and Lahaina Harbor."

"Sure," Luke teased as he reached over and rubbed Sandy's ear. "What could be more boring than the whaling capital of the world? With hundreds of ships and sailors from the seven seas?"

Abby winked at him. "A girl can hope, can't she?"

"Ye'll never be disappointed if ye put yer hope in the Almighty," Duncan said sagely. "Think of all the answered prayers we've seen!"

Luke nodded. "You ought to write them down, Abby. Maybe it'd turn out to be a lively story."

Abby stared at the distant blue horizon. Her hand stopped stroking Sandy, a playful smile tugging at her lips. "I could call it . . . *Luke Quiggley—Hero of the South Seas.*"

When Sandy barked suddenly, they all laughed. "I think she objects," Luke said. "We'd better name it *Abby Captures Hearts Wherever She Goes.*"

"Aye," Duncan said softly, his gray eye meeting Abby's in a tender gaze. "We can all agree on that one."

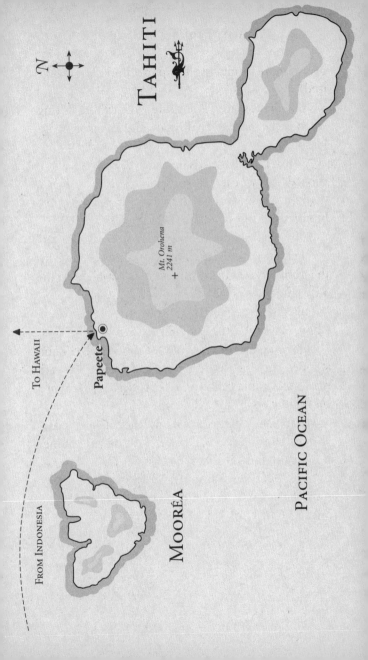

*Don't miss the next exciting adventure in
the South Seas Adventures series:*

Abby
Maui
Mystery

A desperate cry for help and a blazing building
draw Abby and Luke into a dangerous mystery
the minute they return to Maui. Who's fighting
the town's pastor and threatening Abby as she
searches for clues? Will she be able to discover
the arsonist before he strikes again—or kills
her?

Tahitian People, Places, and Words

aita—no

ari'i—royalty or chief

fare tamaa—eating area

fare taoto—sleeping quarters

fare tutu—the kitchen

fiu—fed up

Ia orana or simply *nana*—hello, general greeting (pronounced *yo-rah-nah*)

ma'a—food

mauruuru—thank you

Matavai Bay—on Tahiti, bordered by black sand

Mooréa—an island located in the South Pacific, northwest of Tahiti

Mount Orohena—the tallest mountain on Tahiti

oa oa—happy

panandus—a fiber made from screw-pine leaves and used for woven products such as mats

Papeete—port on Tahiti

pareu (*pareus* for the plural)—two meters of cloth worn in as many ways as you can imagine *poi*—mashed and fermented taro root that is lavender in color

tabu—forbidden

tapa—cloth made from mulberry and used for clothes, mats, etc.

taro—a plant grown in the tropics for its edible rootstocks and in temperate regions for ornament

tiaré—the fragrant, white gardenia flower native to Tahiti

tiki—humanlike sculpture usually made of wood or stone; they can also be a kind of torch

Ua here vau ia oe—I love you (pronounced *oo-ah hay-ray ee-ah oy-ay*)

French Words

au revoir—good-bye

bonjour—good day

merci—thank you

oui—yes

Nautical Words

amidships—in or toward the part of a ship midway between bow and stern

anchor—a device usually of metal attached to a ship by a cable and cast overboard to hold the ship in a particular place

bow—front of ship

bulkhead—raised portion on deck

foredeck—the forepart of a ship's main deck

gangplank—a movable bridge for boarding or leaving a ship at a pier

hatch—a door in the deck of a ship

helm—a lever or wheel used to control the rudder of a ship for steering

porthole—an opening with a cover in the side of a ship

schooner—a sailing vessel with at least two masts

shrouds—a set of ropes that stretch from a ship's side to a masthead

skiff—a small boat

stern—the back of a ship

About the Author

Pamela Walls, author of the South Seas Adventures series, remembers her first scuba dive off the California coast.

"Brr, the water in Monterey Bay is much colder than in Tahiti. But like Luke and Abby, I also had an adventure on my first dive. I saw a leopard shark! The shark was so graceful and beautifully marked that I actually forgot to get scared.

"But 10 minutes later a huge California sea lion came up to investigate. He was adorable, with big black eyes and a doglike head. At first I watched delightedly as he swam like a sleek torpedo through swaying fronds of the golden kelp forest.

"But the sea lion was also six feet long and a little too nosy! It was one thing to admire this sea mammal on TV and another thing to have a giant-sized wild critter—*with teeth*—nosing my rubber flippers. He was as quick as a fish while I, with heavy air tanks strapped to my back, moved like a turtle sloshing around in a washing machine.

"Then when he bit my diving partner's flipper, I began to wonder if there was a specific reason these creatures had been named sea *lions!*

"Another time I was walking the beach in northern California with my girlfriends when we saw 12-foot-long rib bones crashing in the high surf. The largest whale in the world, a blue whale, had died at sea and was washing ashore in pieces. Along with other University of California students, we began collecting the whale's bones. It was smelly work—I lost my appetite for several days. But I'll never forget being able to put my whole hand into one of the whale's blood vessels—a vessel which in you and me might be as tiny as a dandelion stem. When all the bones were collected from that awesome whale, they stretched 100 feet long! You can see the whole skeleton today at Long's Marine Lab, where schoolchildren come to learn about amazing sea creatures.

"Nothing on earth thrills me quite like the ocean. Its mystery, power, and beauty demand my full attention. Especially when I plunge into its depths, because I never know what lies below the surface. Will I find a smiling dolphin or a deadly shark? Will I discover ancient Greek coins or a pirate's sword? But one thing is sure—I will always find some excitement in the deeps, a story that unfolds, or the gift of a seashell, a bone, or a feather on the newly washed beach.

"That's why the sea reminds me of God. The beauty of His words is a gift I carry in my heart. Each day His powerful Spirit washes me clean. And in His depths I find endless possibilities. He writes surprising adventures into the story of my life— with twists and turns that cause me to grow deeper in Him. So every day becomes a new beginning.

"No, nothing in heaven or earth thrills me quite like my God—the Creator of life, wonder, and hope."

May the God of hope fill you with all joy and peace as you trust in Him, so that you may overflow with hope by the power of the Holy Spirit.

Romans 15:13, NIV

WheRe
AdvEnture
beGins
with
a BoOk!

LoG oN @
Cool2Read.com